GEORGE SELDEN

# Harry Cat's
# Pet Puppy

ILLUSTRATED BY
## Garth Williams

A YEARLING BOOK

Published by
Dell Publishing Co., Inc.
1 Dag Hammarskjold Plaza
New York, New York 10017
Text copyright © 1974 by George Selden Thompson
Pictures copyright © 1974 by Garth Williams
All rights reserved. For information address Farrar, Straus &
Giroux, Inc., New York, New York 10003.
Yearling ® TM 913705, Dell Publishing Co., Inc.
Reprinted by arrangement with Farrar, Straus & Giroux, Inc.
Printed in the United States of America
ISBN: 0-440-45647-9

November 1975

10 9 8

MPC

For Barbara and Edward Knowles,
and Sarah, Mary, Emily—
and especially for Christopher!

# CONTENTS

# HARRY CAT'S PET PUPPY

# ONE

# Huppy

"Harry, is that you?" said Tucker Mouse impatiently.

He had his back to the opening of the drainpipe in the Times Square subway station, where he and his friend, Harry Cat, made their home, and he was fixing dinner. Which is to say, he was laying out on a clean part of the floor all the tidbits he had scrounged from around the nearby lunch stand today. They included a scrap of lettuce from a lettuce and tomato sandwich, and a corner of cheese from a ham and cheese sandwich, and a wedge of chocolate from a dropped candy bar.

"I have been waiting, Harry, for *exactly* one hour!" And Tucker Mouse knew that it was *exactly* one hour, because just one week before, the strap of a hapless commuter's watch had broken, and Tucker, ever alert to the value of everything, had dashed out and salvaged the watch before the commuter could find it. "One hour, Harry Cat, and—"

"Come on," whispered Harry gently behind him.

"What do you mean, 'Come on'?" said Tucker. "I'm already here."

"Come on," coaxed Harry.

Tucker turned. "What's *that?*"

In front of Harry, softly urged forward by voice and by nose, was what looked like a dirty dish mop. But this dirty dish mop had four legs and two frightened eyes that kept darting back and forth behind the tangles of knotted hair that fell over its face.

"Get that thing out of here!" shouted Tucker.

"Shh!" warned Harry, under his breath.

"A bit messed up my drainpipe may be," proclaimed Tucker Mouse, "but at least it's not filthy."

"I *said*," said Harry Cat, out loud now and in a tone of voice that Tucker recognized as being don't-argue-with-me serious, "to shut up!" He put a paw on the dish mop's rump and pressed it down. "Just sit now. That's the dog." The mop nervously huddled on its hind legs. "We'll have something to eat."

"It's staying for *supper?*"

"Stop calling him 'it.' It's a puppy—male—and he *is* staying for supper!"

Tucker wiggled his whiskers skeptically. "And just where, may I ask, did you come across this most sterling specimen of the canine species?"

"I found him whimpering—no, not whimpering,

4

crying his heart out—in a dead-end alley on Tenth Avenue."

"A dead-end alley on Tenth Avenue is no place for a puppy to be. Or a mouse, or a cat, or even a human being," agreed Tucker Mouse. "What's its—his—name?"

"He has no name," said Harry. "Whoever threw him away didn't give him a name. And besides, he wouldn't know it anyway. He's too young to talk."

"Well, what's his breed?" demanded Tucker.

"Beats me." Harry looked at the puppy quizzically. "From that hair all over his face there must be some sheep dog in him somewhere. But his shoulders look more like a German shepherd. And that tail—maybe collie, but I don't know."

"It's the melting pot," said Tucker Mouse. He heaved a long sigh. "This is just what I need on a pleasant October day."

He and Harry had come back about a month before from visiting their friend Chester Cricket in Connecticut, and Tucker had been looking forward to an easy and peaceful autumn season. He'd even planned a few trips down to Bryant Park, in back of the Public Library at the corner of Fifth Avenue and Forty-second Street, to enjoy the red and gold colors that made their way into the trees there, even in the midst of all the stone and steel and cement of New York.

"Is that all there is to eat?" said Harry.

6

# Huppy

"One moment!" demanded Tucker. "Even a mouse has manners. We're giving him a shower first."

"Hold on now," objected Harry. "You know how dogs are about baths—"

"He gets not one *scrap* of all the food I have laboriously scrounged for today," announced Tucker, "until he is *clean!* To the shower!—*march!*" With all the authority that a mouse can muster, he propelled the puppy into an opening at the rear of the drainpipe.

In an alcove back there was Tucker's and Harry's shower. From a leaky overhead pipe a steady trickle of water dripped down. And by some miracle the water was *clean*—maybe because it came from one of the pipes leading to the counter of the lunch stand. It filled a hollow in the floor, and then flowed off through a crack in one corner.

Perhaps on the level below his there was another mouse, or a rat, or a cockroach, who was using Tucker's bath water as his own shower—Tucker didn't know or care. Good water is a very valuable commodity in the Times Square subway station. And nobody bothers to ask where it comes from.

"Now into that water and under that shower! Right *now!*" Although the puppy was about four times as big as Tucker himself, the mouse got behind him, put his two front paws on his rump, and gave a tremendous push.

And the puppy went flying into the puddle—where

he there proceeded to sit, beneath the leak, looking as soggy and dismal and sad as a waterlogged puppy can look. "Now soap up!" Tucker undid a piece of Kleenex, took out a clawful of soap chips—scrounged from the lunch stand late one night—and tossed them at the object in his bathtub. And the object just continued to sit—now decorated like a Christmas tree with a lot of snowy chips.

"If I must, I must!" Tucker made the mouse's gesture which, if he'd been a human being, would have been rolling up his sleeves, and marched into the water. Where, with much fuming and fussing, in a couple of minutes he worked up such a lather that both he and the puppy were nothing but two sudsy bubbles.

"Hey, wait a minute!" the Tucker bubble said, and looked back to the entrance to the bathroom, where Harry Cat was sitting contentedly with a smile on his face and his tail curled neatly around his legs. "Why aren't *you* doing this? He's your discovery!"

"But you do it so well," purred Harry. He gave his tail a little snap, and went back into the living room, living drainpipe, that is.

"Well, of all the nerve! Here you drag in—"

"Do hurry though," called Harry. "The puppy and I are getting hungry."

With a vast spluttering and muttering—and not without some soap getting into his eyes—Tucker completed his own and the little dog's shower. Then, from

a niche where the Kleenex and the soap chips were stored, he took two pieces of clean Scot towels—the man who owned the lunch stand could never understand how things just seemed to disappear—and dried them both off.

"Suppertime," he grumbled to the puppy, very resentfully.

But it was suppertime only for Harry and Tucker.

"Whatsa matter with him now?" sulked Tucker Mouse.

The puppy sat miserably, staring down at the lettuce. And the corner of cheese.

"I guess he just doesn't like lettuce," said Harry. "Or cheese, either."

"A gourmet mongrel," moaned Tucker. "Precisely what I didn't need!" His whiskers twitched. "So how do we feed him?"

"I think," began Harry reasonably, "if we wait—"

"I *know!*" announced Tucker in a sudden rodent revelation. "It's *meat!* Dogs like meat." His whiskers flickered thoughtfully. "Now where to get meat?" He went to the opening of the drainpipe and looked out.

It was just past the rush hour. The crazy jumble—it somehow formed itself into a pattern—of commuters going this way and that, which filled the Times Square subway station in the late afternoon, had begun to thin out. There were shoes, legs—all that a mouse could see of human beings—trampling back and forth everywhere. But it wasn't as bad as at five o'clock.

"Meat," murmured Tucker. His twitching whiskers worked on the problem.

"Listen, little Mousiekins—" Harry put his paw gently on Tucker's head and drew it smoothly down his back.

"Don't call me 'Mousiekins'!"

"—when the puppy gets hungry enough, he'll eat."

"Have you ever spent the first weeks of your life in an alley on Tenth Avenue?"

"No, but—"

"So he has to have meat! And tasty meat, too." Tucker silently ran through his categories of tasty meat. His mouth was watering by the time he got to hot dogs, after bits of ham, from ham sandwiches, and—oh joy!—liverwurst. But then the tasty of tasties appeared. "It has to be a hamburger! What more could anybody want?"

"Tucker, he will eat if you'll only—"

"There's an opening! Goodbye."

Before Harry could hold him back, Tucker had spotted a space between the chaotic human beings and made a dash for the lunch stand.

Now a mouse who lives in the Times Square subway station leads a perilous life at best. But one who rushes out openly—though the rush hour may be past—

is taking his four-legged life in his paws. Because in addition to all the commuters, who are only trying to get home, the Times Square subway station is full of transit policemen. Their job is to keep the place as orderly as they can, and they definitely do *not* think of mice as being ornaments of their subway station.

Tucker skittered across the left loafer of a man who was bound for Greenwich, Connecticut, managed to avoid the heel of a lady's shoe, ran right through a transit policeman's legs, and, panting like a sprinter, reached the safety of a corner of the lunch stand.

A middle-aged lady named Louisa was standing at the stove, frying hamburgers and hot dogs. (For the past two years a young man named Mickey, with red curly hair, had tended the lunch stand, but he'd finally saved up enough money and gone off to college this fall. A good thing, too, for the plan Tucker had in mind.)

The mouse caught his breath, and observed Louisa. He'd been observing her for the past two months from the drainpipe opening, and he had decided that she was a nervous type who wouldn't last long in the stress and strife of the Times Square subway station. He intended to make himself a little bit of that stress right now.

Choosing precisely the right moment, when Louisa had just inserted a freshly cooked hamburger between the two halves of a bun, Tucker dashed forward and scratched at her ankle. He was sorry that he ripped her stocking—but first things first. Louisa, startled, looked down and gasped. And then Tucker really did his thing: he jumped up in the air as high as he could, made his grisliest face, wiggled his claws at poor Louisa, and squeaked a little roar that any young lion would have been proud to make.

It worked. Louisa screamed, then shrieked, "A mouse! A rabid mouse!" and began to climb up on the counter beside the stove. And she dropped the hamburger.

Positioning himself like a professional football player, Tucker caught the burger, and holding it in both arms—it was far too big to fit under just one— he began some broken-field running back to the drainpipe.

And got there! Although his tail did get stepped on by a perfectly innocent man from Iowa who just wanted to see what Times Square looked like.

"Look, Harry! Look, Harry! I got—"

"You fool! You could've been killed!"

"Yeah, but *look*, Harry! I got this hamburger. And she's a *big* one, too!" Tucker cuddled his hamburger, half out of hunger—he was hoping there'd be a little morsel left over—but mostly out of pride.

As it happened, there was not one morsel left over. As soon as Tucker set the hamburger down, and lifted off the top half of the bun, and the puppy smelled the steaming meat beneath, that little dog discovered that he was starved. As well he might be, since the last thing he'd had to eat was a sliver of rotten boloney discovered in the gutter of Tenth Avenue.

"Well, that takes care of that," said Tucker glumly, staring at the space where the hamburger meat had been.

"Come on," said Harry. "We still have the bun. And it's laced with lovely meat juice."

Tucker consoled himself with that thought, and was almost through his half of the bun when he noticed that Harry wasn't eating. *"Now* what's wrong?" he demanded through juicy lips.

"He's crying," said Harry quietly.

Tucker jerked up his mouth. "He's—"

Over in one corner, his head leaning on the wall, eyes hidden behind his scraggly hair, but the tears dropping down nonetheless, the puppy sat, all alone.

"Come on," coaxed Harry, in a voice soft as his fur. "Come on. Come here. Be part of our party."

The puppy came up and sat beside Harry.

"That's right," said Harry. It may seem very strange that a cat should do this, but with his nails withdrawn he reached out and petted and stroked the dog's head. "You're Harry's pet puppy. Harry's puppy. All right?"

"Hh-hhh—"

"He's starting to say something!" burst in Tucker Mouse.

"Shh. *Shh!*" Harry warned.

"Hu-huppy," stuttered the dog.

"Harry's puppy. Huppy." Harry glanced toward his friend. "Okay with you? That we call him that?"

Tucker looked at the two of them, his whiskers dripping with now forgotten delicious meat juice. "Okay with me. I guess."

# TWO

# The Nuisance

But a few days later Tucker wasn't so sure it was all okay.

"Tuppy," he grumbled. "It could have been 'Tuppy.' Tucker's puppy. After all, *I* scrounged up that hamburger!"

A pet puppy, the next few weeks were to prove, could be a nuisance. Especially when its true master was out prowling—which is a cat's duty as well as his pleasure—through the vast mechanical labyrinth of the city of New York.

There was, for instance, the very day after the puppy moved in, the question of—

"Stop that!" shouted Tucker Mouse. "You stop that right now! Come over here!"

In the farthest corner of the drainpipe, and discreetly concealed behind a big chunk of fallen plaster that Harry had pushed into position, was a section of floor that was always covered with several layers of very clean newspaper. Late each night, when the subway was almost empty and safe, either Tucker or Harry—they took turns at the chore—would wrap the newspapers up, secure them with a rubber band, and deposit them in a nearby trash basket. (Tucker always made sure that he'd scrounged up a sufficient supply of rubber bands. The take-out department of the lunch counter was very handy for that.)

"Now *there*," said Tucker Mouse, with all the parental authority he could muster, as he pointed down at the newspaper, "is where you do—what you have to do." He marched grandly back into the living area of the drainpipe.

And in a few minutes Huppy slouched back, too.

"Do we have that all straight now?" demanded the mouse.

"Yup," muttered Huppy. He had a few words now. A very few.

But he didn't understand at all. Anyone who has raised a pet puppy will know what a trial the first few weeks are. They were an especially difficult trial for Tucker Mouse, who prided himself on having the very cleanest—if still chaotic—drainpipe in the Times Square subway station.

"Harry," he said that night, when the big striped cat got back from his roaming and roving, and Huppy was asleep, "we have to talk about something."

"I can guess," said Harry with a sniff. He could see

that much of the living area had been rearranged, and that a commuter's handkerchief—a favorite from Tucker's collection of human salvages—had been thrown out.

"It is absolutely *ridiculous* for a mouse to toilet-train a dog." Tucker drew himself up to his full regal height—about three inches. "I will not appear ridiculous."

"Well, if that's all that's worrying you, Mousiekins," said Harry Cat, "you don't need to worry, because you have never failed to be—"

"*And don't give me any of your furry lip!*" shouted Tucker as his three inches collapsed.

"Easy now," soothed Harry. "It'll just take time. You know how puppies are."

"No, I *don't* know how puppies are!" growled Tucker in a mouse's growl. "Me being perhaps the first mouse in recorded history that had to take care of one!" He kicked a belt buckle he'd salvaged a week before. "And by the way—as far as taking care of goes—"

"I've been busy," said Harry.

"A cat's excuse," grumbled Tucker Mouse. "Always the same excuse. 'Been busy . . .' Doing *what?*"

Harry Cat didn't answer. He was trying to formulate a plan, but he wasn't ready to discuss it yet.

Instead of replying to Tucker's question, he went over and looked at the sleeping puppy. And tucked a Kleenex—a special Kleenex, because Tucker had managed to salvage it whole—beneath the little dog's left shoulder.

"He keeps kicking it off," fretted Tucker Mouse. He ran around to the other side and fastidiously edged the torn fringe in. He had meant to use the Kleenex for some grand and glorious nose-blowing. But although it was a blanket now—he'd decided that an hour ago, on a chilly fall evening, when he put Huppy to bed—he demanded that at least it be treated with respect.

Though less undignified than his toilet-training, another of Huppy's habits caused Tucker much more worry.

One Tuesday, between the early rush hour and lunchtime, Tucker looked up from a morning chore— the counting of his life savings, making sure that none had been stolen—to find that the puppy was gone.

"Huppy?" he anxiously asked the empty drainpipe. "Huppy—are you here?"

He was not.

"Huppy? . . . *Huppy!*" A panicky feeling began to climb up Tucker's chest. He ran to the drainpipe opening. And there, not three feet away, snuffling contentedly at the base of an overflowing trash basket, was a nonchalant dish mop. "Come *back* in here!" The dish mop ambled into the drainpipe. "Don't you *ever* go out there again!" After all, the Times Square subway station was not exactly a tended lawn, with a high protective fence around it. It was a madness of comings and goings, and busy, thoughtless human beings.

"Now I mean it!" Tucker lectured sternly. "*I* will decide when you're old enough to go out in the world."

"Rrff," said Huppy begrudgingly.

But Tucker Mouse did *not* decide when Huppy went out in the world again. He went out that same afternoon, having smelled a delectable hunk of frankfurter in the trash basket nearest the subway tracks.

"Huppy!" shouted Tucker, after a frantic search through the drainpipe. "Don't go near the edge!" He darted out—a flash of gray fur—and began to pull the dog by his ears. But, young as he was, Huppy was much too big for the mouse. And much too obstinate. He just sat down and let his floppy ears be pulled.

"Oh, please," begged Tucker, "come home! Huppy,

*please!*" It was almost four-thirty—the time when the tramping feet began. "I'll get that hot dog, I *promise* I will!"

Huppy let his ears be dragged back to safety. And true to his word, Tucker skittered out into the open again and salvaged what turned out to be an almost inedibly old piece of hot dog.

"To think"—Tucker leaned against the drainpipe and panted—"for that lousy little chunk of meat, I risked extinction."

In the next few days, against his wishes and his express commands, Tucker risked extinction many times. Because Huppy had found a delightful game. It happened that if he ran out into the subway station—and better still, cavorted out there, jumped up and down, and had lots of fun—this hysterical mouse would dash right after him, and plead, and pull ears, which didn't hurt, and push him from the rump, and do just about anything to get him back into that hole in the wall. Which the mouse kept calling "home."

"I can't stand it!" said Tucker Mouse one night. That afternoon Huppy had not only run all the way to the other side of the station—beyond the end of the shuttle tracks, and his farthest excursion yet—he had also hidden himself behind a trash basket and barked at a transit policeman: great sport!

"This is serious," said Harry Cat. His forehead puckered up in a frown until his eyebrows touched.

"He could have been caught. Or even killed, if he fell on the shuttle tracks."

"*He* could have been killed! *He* could—! What about—"

"Mousiekins—" Harry pacified his friend, as he usually did, by putting a heavy paw on his back and gently flattening him on the floor.

"Harry, please," Tucker gasped. "If you wouldn't mind not squashing me—"

"—you know every hole in this subway station," the cat went on. "You know every crack. You could *escape*. But Huppy's young. He doesn't understand danger yet."

"Young he may be," said Tucker Mouse. "But heavy he's also getting. I had to practically *carry* him back here, before that cop could find where the barking was coming from."

The cat frowned again. "Really serious. And I haven't decided what to do."

"About what?" asked Tucker.

"Never mind," said Harry. "Let's wake him up. This business of misbehaving and running around—we've got to have it out right now."

They went over to what was now called "Huppy's House." It was a fairly large cardboard box—which had originally contained six bottles of Scotch whiskey, and which Harry had found, by the greatest good luck, late one night in the street and dragged all the way down to the subway station. He and Tucker had to bend it a little to fit it through the drainpipe opening, but they'd managed it without too much damage. Then, the next Sunday, working together, the two of them had salvaged a copy of the Sunday *New York Times,* and Tucker had shredded the whole thing by claw— which was quite a job, since the Sunday *Times* is about as big as a newspaper can get. And *then*—the climax of "Huppy's House"—Tucker discovered a ripped but still usable cushion in one of the trash baskets. After inspecting it thoroughly, to make sure that no bugs or other unwelcome guests were living in it, Tucker fitted it into one end of the box, so Huppy had a place to lay his head. Tucker waited for thanks, but the little dog just sniffed it and said, "Woof." But he lay down right away and fell asleep with his head resting on it. And looked quite nice, Tucker thought. At first the box had seemed much too big for the puppy, but he'd grown so rapidly, just in the time he'd been living with Tucker and Harry, that now it fitted him perfectly.

"Wake up. Come on—" Harry reached inside and shook the puppy. He grumbled in his sleep. "—wake *up!*"

Huppy stumbled up to a sitting position. His head barely reached to the top of the box's side. "Wha'—?" "Wha'" was another of the few words he'd learned.

Harry gave him a very stern lecture—complete with

gestures and demonstrations of running around, just in case Huppy couldn't understand everything—which ended with "Mustn't!" He shook his furry paw in warning. *"Mustn't!* Bad dog! Mustn't do! Now promise! You promise?"

The little dog hung his head and his eyes peered out, cowed, through his tangle of hair. "Yup, Hawy," he murmured, and dropped back down onto his pillow. In a minute his soft little snores could be heard.

"I think that should do it," said Harry Cat, rather pleased with the feline authority that he exercised over a growing dog.

"I hope so—*Hawy!*" sulked Tucker Mouse.

That was *another* thing that made Tucker mad. Huppy refused to call him by name. By his third week in the drainpipe he was adding words fast. There was "hammaga" for hamburger; there was "fwamps" for frankfurters; there was "swa," for coleslaw. (Tucker could see by this time where the heart of a little dog lies: it lies right in his mouth.) There was "yup" and "nope"—picked up from a conductor on the shuttle, and obstinately retained, despite all Tucker Mouse's efforts to make him say "yes" and "no"—and one glorious afternoon there was "Hawy."

The two had been playing together, Harry half tickling and half wrestling with Huppy. And suddenly, out of nowhere—which is where a lot of words come from to puppies and other young people—the little dog stopped his giggling and rolling around, looked up at the smiling cat, and said solemnly, "Hawy." It wasn't a question; he wasn't asking for anything. He simply had found Harry's name. There's a mystery in names, something very important—and especially the names of living things: names make things be themselves.

And when Huppy said, "Hawy," the cat and the mouse just looked at each other. Tucker Mouse had been sitting on the sidelines, wondering if he should join in the fun, and had just about decided to, when it happened. But instead, for a moment, they both sat silently, recognizing what a great thing had happened.

However, in the opinion of Tucker Mouse the moment would have been even greater—far greater, in fact —if, after "Hawy," the dog had said, "Tucka"—or anything else that sounded like him. But Huppy did not. He went on wrestling with the big gentle cat, repeating over and over again, "Hawy! Hawy! Hawy!" and laughing hilariously . . . Tucker decided not to join in.

But the very next day, when Harry was out—he wouldn't have dreamed of admitting to a twinge of jealousy—the mouse spent one whole afternoon coaxing, asking, pleading, and at last demanding that Huppy say his name.

He pointed at the puppy and then himself—"You Huppy, me Tucker"—like a pioneer trying to teach an Indian to speak English.

# The Nuisance

"Hammaga!" said Huppy.

"Me Tucker!"

"Fwamps!"

"No, *Tucker!*" the mouse shouted. "Tucker Mouse. Now *say* it!"

"Hawy!" The puppy began to snicker. Then, adding insult to injury, he said, "Hawy *Cat!*"—and rolled over on his back, squeaking with glee and scratching the empty air with his paws. It was something that he only did when he was especially pleased with himself. Like the times when he gave Tucker Mouse a fit.

That night, when the wrestling started again, Tucker wouldn't even watch.

The last straw, the straw that broke the mouse's back, dropped into place like an iron crowbar late one Thursday afternoon about a month after Huppy's arrival. (And he still would not speak Tucker's name.)

The last Thursday of every month—the mouse always salvaged a calendar in January of each new year—was house-cleaning day in the drainpipe. That meant, for all practical purposes, that Tucker rearranged the clutter of everything that he'd ever collected. He promised Harry every month that he would get rid of the useless possessions, but Tucker had one of those hoarding souls that couldn't bear to lose a thing. So he moved all the junk to new locations—at least it made the drainpipe *look* different—and called it cleaning house. And each month, with an aching heart full of pride, he did throw away something—but only so he could say to Harry, "Well, I got rid of *that*, didn't I?" Four weeks ago it had been a shoelace—horrible loss!— that he put back into the same trash basket that he'd pulled it out of the day before, and this month—this month—Tucker looked around. The broken glasses had to stay—a real prize, that—and so did the brass belt buckle. But at last he decided that with a great effort of will he could stand to be separated from a hairpin he'd found two weeks ago. With a heavy sigh he threw it out the drainpipe opening, and hoped that some young lady might find it, and wash it, and use it. It wasn't that he was completely a miser—he was a bit of a one, to be sure—but Tucker also couldn't bear the thought of anything being simply wasted.

Huppy had watched him all afternoon, lugging this thing here, and that thing there, and the other thing into the opposite corner. (It was really redecorating, not cleaning at all.) And the puppy had been most impressed when Tucker said to himself, "I guess I can throw this out"—and tossed the hairpin to what- ever fate awaited it. But the effort, mental—*losing things!*—as well as physical—moving everything around —left the mouse exhausted. He crawled into his corner, fluffed up his shredded newspapers, and took a much needed nap.

# The Nuisance

And woke up an hour later to the most horrendous experience in his entire life!

In a dream he thought he heard jingling. It was a sound that Tucker liked because it reminded him of the time each day when he counted his life savings: the loose change, most precious of all his possessions, that was neatly piled in a hole in the drainpipe wall. But then, for some reason—perhaps because he couldn't *feel* the coins—the jingling began to worry him.

His eyes opened—just in time to see Huppy's tail going out the drainpipe opening. "Hey! Come back!" Tucker jumped up, grabbed a clawful of tail, and dragged the puppy back inside. "You've been told, by your friend 'Hawy'—"

The mouse didn't finish his scolding. Because just then Huppy, whose cheeks looked funny to Tucker— kind of bulging—gave a cough, and out of his mouth dropped three quarters, four dimes, and six nickels.

*"What on earth!"*

Tucker stared at the coins for a second. Then whirled around—and his worst suspicions were confirmed. The piece of plaster that concealed the hole in the wall where he kept his life savings, and which he carefully replaced every day after counting it all, had been pushed aside. Half his money was gone. If he'd had the time, Tucker Mouse would have fainted dead away on the spot. But within his panic a warning

sounded: something more might be wrong. And it was! Almost all his other possessions were gone as well. The drainpipe was practically empty.

"What have you been *doing*?" he screamed.

"Th'o away! Th'o away!" beamed Huppy happily. In his innocence, having watched Tucker move all his belongings around, and having been especially impressed when Tucker heaved the hairpin out, he'd decided that, well, it would be a good idea if he threw away everything else. Particularly those shiny things in that hole.

"Oh, my lord—" Tucker clutched his chest and fought off a heart attack. Then his panic turned into action—and anger. "Get in that box! And *stay* there! No supper tonight, you stupid *mutt!*"

Trembling, Huppy jumped in his house and hid his head under the pillow. He just thought he'd been helping.

One of the few things not thrown out—yet—was the wrist watch. Four o'clock. Half an hour before the human herds began their stampede through the station.

Tucker turned into a furry whirlwind. Throwing caution completely aside—what was life without his life savings?—he dashed out into the subway station. And in half an hour of mad scrambling he'd retrieved two dollars and eighty-three cents—naturally, he went after the money first—and many of the furnishings. (Luckily, Huppy was still quite small, and he hadn't been able to throw things too far from the drainpipe opening.)

But much was lost. When the commuters did begin their rush, Tucker could only sit in the drainpipe opening, in a daze of fury and pain, and look on hopelessly as they picked up missing nickels, dimes, and quarters that he knew belonged to him.

Harry Cat got back late that night. But Tucker was definitely *not* asleep. In a flurry of sputtering, swearing, stamping, he managed to tell the dreadful tale.

"Now take it easy, Tucker." Harry knew that this was more than serious. For Tucker Mouse it was downright drastic—and might even prove fatal. "He's just—"

"I don't care *what* he's just!" Tucker roared hysterically. "Besides my life savings—my buckle—my high heel—!"

"I'll slip down to Fifth Avenue and steal you a *pair* of high-heel shoes," Harry promised.

"I don't *want* a pair of high-heel shoes! I want my good old heel. And it's gone! I saw some dope kick it onto the tracks."

"We'll talk about this—"

"We'll talk about this right now." Tucker pointed a shaking claw at the cardboard box—from which a peep had not been heard all night. "He goes!"

"Shh!" warned Harry. "You'll wake him up."

"This is *my* house!" Tucker whispered indignantly. "And he goes! Tomorrow!"

"Well, where does he go?" asked Harry, as calmly as he could.

"To Bellevue Hospital if necessary! They *need* animals over there. They experiment on them!"

"*Tucker!*"

"I mean it, Harry! We could sell him there. I could get back the ninety-five cents he still owes me—"

Hurt, worried, and deeply disappointed, the cat

32

HALF DOZEN

BEST SC

WHIS

SPEC

turned his back coldly on his friend. "I will not discuss this further tonight."

"Discuss it or not, tomorrow he goes!" In a rush of rage Tucker kicked Huppy's house. It shivered, then fell still. "The stupid, vicious little mutt!"

# THREE

# A Cold and Rainy, Wretched Day

"It's raining," stated Tucker Mouse the next morning. An hour of nobody speaking to anybody could drive a mouse mad—especially one with a guilty conscience. Through the maze of pipes that led up to the grating on the sidewalk above, he could hear a faint patter. At least it was something to talk about. "Harry?" he almost pleaded. "It's raining."

"I can hear." The cat lay in the same position, paws outstretched, eyes narrowed to a slit, in which he had woken up.

"What are you thinking about?" Tucker asked plaintively.

"I was wondering when the best time would be to take Huppy to Bellevue. To the vivisection department."

"Oh, Harry, stop it!" the mouse shouted, as if he was trying to stop something—a memory maybe—within himself. "I didn't mean that."

"You said that."

"But I didn't *mean* it, Harry. I haven't slept a wink all night. I apologize, Harry—I really do. Not a moment's rest, all night."

Harry Cat sat up. "Well, if *you* can apologize, I guess there's hope for all of us." The two of them looked at each other. And a wall had fallen down. But Harry's tail switched nervously. "I still don't know what to do, though."

"Oh, don't worry about my things," said Tucker magnanimously. "Last night I found sixty more cents—and my two best buttons—oh, and the belt buckle too!"

"I might have known," sighed Harry. "Didn't sleep all night—and I thought you were sorry—"

"I *am* sorry, Harry. But to pass the time, since I couldn't drop off—and the subway was almost empty—"

"Okay, okay. So you're not a ruined mouse any more. What I meant was—what are we going to do about—" He jerked his head toward Huppy's house, from which a peep had still not come. Harry went on softly, not to wake late sleepers up, "I still haven't found a place for him."

"A place?" Tucker didn't understand.

"Look, Mousiekins, what do you think I've been doing for the past two months? Just frolicking on the town all this time? I've been looking for a home for Huppy!" Tucker dropped back on his haunches; that thought had never occurred to him. "A *permanent* home! He can't live in this drainpipe forever. It's all right for a cat and a mouse. A growing dog?—no! But I haven't come up with a single thing."

"Dumb me. A permanent home." Tucker twitched his whiskers, thinking. "I wonder where he'd like to live."

"Let's ask him," said Harry "Sooner or later we would have had to, anyway." He went over to Huppy's house, reared back on his hind legs, and rested his forepaws on the rim of the box. And turned into a petrified statue of a cat. *"Tucker!"*

The mouse jumped up onto one corner of the box, and he too froze there, balanced, two legs on one side and two on the other. "He's gone!"

"When?"

"Oh, Harry, it's all my fault—"

"But *when* could—"

"Last night—"

"—he have run away?"

"—I was chasing all over the subway station, looking for all those—"

"Oh, Huppy—"

"—lousy little things, and—and—"

They were jabbering at one another as if they were rabid, hardly hearing a thing that the other said.

"It *is* my fault!" Tucker toppled back down on the drainpipe floor, hoping that he would hurt himself. "He must have been awake all the time, and heard me say Bellevue, and experimenting on animals—"

Harry was first to get back his sanity. "Now stop, Tucker—"

"—and I called him a vicious little mutt—oh! oh! oh!" The mouse hid his eyes in his claws. But he still saw himself as he'd acted last night.

"I say *stop!* Right now! You be guilt-ridden later. We both have to *think!* Where's he gone? Where'd he hide? Then we have to go find him!"

There passed ten minutes of quick, alternating thoughts—mostly those of Harry Cat, because Tucker couldn't wait to feel guilty—as they tried to decide where the dog had gone. The nearest entrance to the subway station led up to the east side of Broadway. He must have gone that way. They both were convinced he'd left the station.

"Too frightened we'd find him here," moaned Tucker, "and take him—"

"Shut up!" said Harry Cat.

They dashed up through a roundabout path of pipes—to avoid all the people on the entrance stairs—and arrived on the sidewalk. A cold gray rain, which would have been snow if the temperature was a little lower, was punishing New York for something.

"Now looking west," Harry thought out loud. The dog would have seen, past the old Times Tower, the crowded block between Seventh and Eighth avenues. Lights blinking outside movie theaters, cars coming and going, brakes screeching, horns honking, the crush of restless human beings. "That probably would have scared him."

But eastward—less noise, less lights, less people. He might even have caught a glimpse, beneath the street lights, a block away, of the tops of the trees in Bryant Park. "Come on! Down here," the cat commanded, and crouching low, they scuttled through the streaming gutter toward the Avenue of the Americas. Under each parked car they stopped and shouted, as loud as they dared, "Huppy! Huppy?" And got back in answer nothing but the indifferent city sounds.

On a pleasant day Bryant Park can be a truly beautiful, natural place: a living rectangle of grass and trees in the midst of a city conjured of concrete and steel. But today, with bare branches dripping, it felt desolate and unprotected. And it was empty—except for Lulu.

"Hi, you guys!" she called down from a branch.

"This is all we need," whispered Tucker to Harry. "To meet that kookoo bird."

"Oh, Lulu's okay," Harry whispered back. "As a matter of fact, she can help us."

Now Lulu Pigeon was definitely not a cuckoo. But she was, as she freely admitted herself, a rather kookoo bird. She came from a very distinguished pigeon clan that claimed to be descended from the original Hynrik Stuyvesant Pigeons. And they claimed to have come to New York clinging to the yardarm of a Dutch sailing vessel, when New York was still New Amsterdam. But over the years the Stuyvesant Pigeons and their descendants had grown very grand indeed. You might even say snooty. They refused to be seen below Fourteenth Street. However, every family—birds, too—has at least one flap-out. And a year ago Lulu flapped out of the private Stuyvesant Pigeon tree uptown and came down to live in Bryant Park— "Nearer where the action is really at!" she explained. She called everybody "guys," or "men," or "fellas," no matter what kind of animal it was—her talk, in fact, was the latest New York slang—and within a few months she'd established herself as one of the authentic characters in the Times Square area.

"What are you cats doing out today?" (She also called everybody "cats," even if it was a dog or a mouse.)

Harry explained how he and Tucker had adopted Huppy—"Ooo, that's groovy!" cooed Lulu, who still had some pigeon left in her speech—and then how Huppy had run away. "Bad day for splitting." Lulu shook her head. "Only out here myself to hunt up a seed or two."

"Will you help us find him?" Harry asked.

"Sure, men." Lulu coasted down through the air and settled next to them. "Love to!"

The plan, rapidly decided upon, was this: Tucker and Harry should continue on down the south side of

## A Cold and Rainy, Wretched Day

Forty-second Street, and Lulu—"Since I got wings!"
she boastfully flapped, and so could search out nooks
and crannies and doorways more quickly—Lulu Pigeon
would take on the north side herself.

"All the way to the East River, if necessary!" said
Harry.

An excellent idea, they all agreed. There was one
thing wrong, though: it didn't work. Nobody found
Huppy. And four hours later, having peeked in every
possible place where a little dog might hide, they were
back in Bryant Park—drenched, shivering, and discon-
solate.

"Too bad the other dogs aren't around," said Lulu.
"They could help."

"What other dogs?" asked Tucker.

"There's a pack that hangs out around the park here.
Some pretty tough guys, too. But on days like this—or
when the cops are makin' a sweep—they hole up in
cellars all over the city."

"There's nothing to do," said Harry Cat, "but tackle
that block between Seventh and Eighth. He might have
thought, if he got in a theater, he'd be safe in the dark,
and be warm."

"And see a flick too!" added Lulu.

"I doubt very much if movies were on his mind!"
said Harry. "Come on!"

They switched sides of the street this time—with the
same result: nothing. By evening they were back in the

park. The gray day was dying, defeated by night. But the rain had grown stronger—had turned into sleet.

"You didn't see *any* dogs?" asked Harry.

"Not a hair of a one," said Lulu. "But I caught the last half of the *greatest* Roadrunner cartoon! He was in this tunnel, with a Mack truck bearing down on him—"

"*Lulu!*" Tucker shouted. "Did you take time off to look at the movies?"

"Well, Mousiekins, I was in the theater, so—"

"And don't call me Mousiekins! Only Harry can call me that."

"He can? Since when?"

"No, he can't! But he's the only one who can!"

"Will you two *please* keep quiet?" said Harry. His teeth were chattering. So were Tucker's. And so was Lulu Pigeon's beak. "Now I *really* have to think." He paced, and stopped. "If I was Huppy—" And paced, and stopped. "—if I was a dog—who lived in a drainpipe—and was only acquainted with the Times Square subway station—" Abruptly he pounced on an idea he'd had. "Of course! That's it! How stupid can an alley cat get? Follow me!"

Tucker, spluttering, and Lulu, fluttering, followed Harry as he ran down Forty-first Street, avoiding the crowds on Forty-second. The cat panted out an explanation. "The subway—*isn't* the only place—Huppy knows!" Tucker tripped, fell into a puddle, and swore. "He *must* remember—where I found him!"

Across Eighth—across Ninth—they reached Tenth Avenue. "Now if *I* can only remember where that dismal, filthy alley was—"

"Shall we fan out again?" asked Lulu Pigeon.

"No. I'm sure it's—it's—*here!*" Harry suddenly stopped. A black corridor that was darker than the coming night yawned threateningly between two buildings. The only thing the three could see, through the sleet, in the dim glow that a street light cast, was the outline of a garbage can.

"We gotta go in *there?*" said Lulu.

"You don't have to go anywhere," Harry answered. "But I'm—"

"After me!" In a fit of courage very unlike himself—unless he was after something really valuable, like a high heel or a belt buckle—Tucker scooted past his friend, and vanished. Very catlike and quick, on the pads of his feet, Harry followed him.

"Oh, well," said the bird, "if I gotta, I gotta." She flapped into the dark. But after she'd almost brained herself on a brick wall she couldn't see, she decided she'd better land and walk.

"Huppy? Huppy? Huppy?"

He wasn't behind the first garbage can. Or the second. Or the third. As they felt their way into the pitch-black alley, nobody could see a thing—not even each other. They reached the end: a final wall across their path.

"He's not here"—Tucker Mouse.

"He's got to be!"—Harry Cat.

"Let's get outa this place!"—Lulu Pigeon. "I got a feeling there's *something* there—like maybe meat-eating rats!"

"Ah—"

"Shh!"—Harry Cat again.

"What?"—Tucker Mouse.

"Ah-*choo!*"

"That's him!" said Harry.

Tucker dashed toward the sneeze. "I got him! He's here—"

"Let go! Let go!" a voice whimpered.

"Don't scare him!" warned Harry.

" 'Bye, boys," said Lulu. "I'll wait for you all in the street."

Coaxing, cajoling—and finally carrying—Tucker and Harry got Huppy out to the sidewalk's edge. "Oh, I'm *so* glad we found him! I'm *so* glad we found him," the mouse kept moaning.

But the puppy huddled against Harry Cat. "Now don't be afraid," Harry purred reassuringly. "We're going home."

Which they did—after introducing Lulu. She shook her head. "Poor bedraggled mutt."

"Don't you call him a mutt!" said Tucker.

For if the three of them were drenched, then Huppy was absolutely flooded. Like a soggy sponge he squished along beside Harry, back to the Times Square subway station.

"You're welcome to stay overnight," said Harry.

"No, thanks," said Lulu. "There's a guy down on Second Avenue who owns an antique shop. He doesn't know a back window is busted. I sack out down there in weather like this. But I'll drop in later on, this week, to see how the"—she glanced at Tucker—"the little dog is." And flew off through the winter night.

A time of frantic drying began. Using shredded newspapers, Kleenex, Scot towels, anything they could get their claws or paws on, the cat and the mouse rubbed Huppy dry. Then they fed him—only a chunk of cheese, all they had, but he ate it gratefully—and Harry punched up the pillow so it was good and soft.

"Wait!" said Tucker. "Last night—I saw something—" He whisked out into the subway station, and came back a minute later dragging a piece of red-checked flannel shirt behind him. "Tuck him in."

"*You* tuck him in!" said Harry Cat. "That's your name, isn't it?"

"That's a lousy joke," said Tucker. But he jumped at the chance—jumped, in fact, right into Huppy's house, and began to tuck him in like mad. "Now soon you'll be nice and warm," he soothed.

"Thank you, Tucka."

"*Harry!*" The mouse beamed up at Harry Cat, who was on his hind legs, looking down.

"I know. I heard."

"Tucka *Mouse!*" said Huppy, and laughed to himself.

Tucker *Mouse* jumped out of the cardboard box. And looked away.

A minute passed. Then, "Well," said Harry, "you glad he's back?"

"I'm glad," said Tucker.

"And what's that on your cheek?"

"It's nothing." Tucker brushed nothing away. "Some rain."

"We've been home an hour."

"A little leftover rain, is all."

# FOUR

# A Growing Dog

"Ah-*choo!*"

That first sneeze in the alley was just the beginning. The sleet, the cold—Huppy got sick. But Harry and Tucker just thought it was sniffles. They had no idea how ill he was until Lulu came calling a few days after they'd gotten the little dog back.

She flew through the station, waddled into the drain-pipe, took one look at Huppy, shivering in his box, and said, "That's a very sick dog. Feel his nose!"

"Why his nose?" demanded Tucker Mouse.

"You can tell if he has a temperature. The hotter the nose, the higher the fever."

"Since when were you a veterinarian, Lulubelle?" asked Harry.

"Ooo, I know all about dogs," said Lulu. "Max—he's the head of the pack that meets in Bryant Park—Max tells me everything."

Tucker jumped into Huppy's house. "His nose is burning up."

"Pneumonia, probably," cooed the pigeon.

"Thanks a lot!" said Tucker. But he began to worry.
The next day he worried even more, because
Huppy's nose was hotter still. And back came Lulu,
with more cheery information. "Max says there's nothing that you can do. He says he eats a special grass when
he's sick. But it's winter now, and the grass is dead."

"Well, I think there's something to do," said Harry.
"We'll keep him warm, and give him lots to eat and
drink—he'll be well in a week."

"Hope so," said Lulu. "Toodle-oo!"

Huppy was *not* well in a week. If anything, he was
worse. Harry tried to stay calm, although he too, behind a hopeful smile, was extremely concerned. Some-

one *had* to stay calm, because Tucker was frantic—more frantic, that is, than usual. He would feel just as guilt-ridden if the dog died of pneumonia as he would if they hadn't been able to find him at all. And he ran around the drainpipe, as Harry Cat said, feeling Huppy's nose every hour, "like a hysterical head nurse." Harry sneaked a touch himself every now and then, when Tucker was out scrounging up something for Huppy to eat.

And if as a nurse the mouse overdid it somewhat, in the matter of food he proved himself a hero. Like most sick people, Huppy had no appetite, and to get him the goodies that went down most easily, Tucker risked life, limb, and dignity. He found that the one thing that *always* was welcome was *un*melted ice cream. The soup left over when a chunk had melted was not enough; Huppy liked to lap at the sweet solid cold. Very natural too, Nurse Tucker decided, for someone who had a fever. But rushing the stuff in a paper cup all the way back to the drainpipe late at night when the lunch stand had closed was quite a task. (Fortunately, the cover to the vanilla ice-cream container did not quite fit.)

It was when Huppy began to ask for strawberry that Harry suspected he was getting better. He was sure of it one morning after Tucker had taken his temperature for the tenth time that day and Harry had told him to for heaven's sake lay off!—and the dog airily allowed, "Oh, that's all right, Harry. Tucker can hold my nose if he wants to." (At least, after all these weeks —it already was January—Huppy had his "r's" by now.)

"He can, can he—mhmm," Harry purred. "I think instead of nose-holding what you need now is a little fresh air."

"Fresh air!" shrieked Tucker. "You want him to get pneumonia again?"

"And since we're having a thaw right now, I believe we'll go up to the sidewalk tonight and get you at least ten good breaths. All right?"

"No, Harry!"

"All right." When Harry Cat agreed with himself, the argument was settled. He didn't want Huppy to become a chronic invalid. Which is often what happens when a sick youngster who is getting better is fed too much ice cream.

So that night—after Tucker had tried, and failed, to tie the piece of flannel shirt around the puppy with a piece of precious string—they set out for the sidewalk.

Set out, that is, two steps. Then Harry and Tucker froze in their tracks and stared at each other. The dog couldn't fit through the opening!

"Harry—he's grown—"

"Hawy!"

"Now don't be scared. And don't forget your r's,"

said the cat. "You worked hard on them. We'll get you out of here." Neither he nor Tucker had noticed how *much* the puppy had grown. "That darned ice cream!" thought Harry—along with the hamburgers and the franks and everything else that Tucker had stuffed into him. "We'll just have to use the back way—through the pipes."

It wasn't that easy, however. The back hole to the drainpipe was larger than the front—and Huppy got through it without too much trouble—but a few feet in, the pipe split. The way that Tucker and Harry usually took to the street was too small. They had to turn left—the first of many left turns—when they should have turned right, and turn downward when they should have turned up. After half an hour they'd gone so far, and in so many different directions, that even Harry didn't know where they were—but it felt as if they ought to be in Brooklyn by now!

The cat was leading the way—if fumbling in darkness through unknown pipes could be called leading—Huppy inching behind him, with Tucker Mouse bringing up the rear. "Let's take a rest," said Harry, and stopped. In the cramped pitch-black no one said a word. Then Huppy began to whimper. Harry twisted around and pawed the air till he found the dog's head, which he patted. "I *promise* you, Huppy, I'll get you out."

"No, you won't! I'll get bigger and bigger—pretty

soon I won't even be able to move—I'll squash myself to death!"

"Let's get going!" came Tucker's anxious voice from behind.

"You two stay here," said Harry. "I'm going on ahead and scout."

Huppy couldn't turn around and Tucker couldn't squeeze past him, so he did the best he could by patting the puppy's rump and telling him it would be all right—which he hoped but wasn't at all sure of.

Neither one of them heard the cat come back. "It's always worse right near the end. Two left—one down, one up—then a long level right and we're on the street. And you'll never guess where we come out!"

"North Dakota!" said Tucker.

They came out on the corner of Forty-first Street and Broadway—exactly one block from the entrance to the subway station. But the night was so beautiful, when they'd found a deserted doorway to sit in, that it almost made up for all their effort. A January thaw—like spring in midwinter—is a fragile, strange season. The air was clear, a warm wind brushed the animals' fur, and high above, the remote bright stars seemed far more pure than the city's glitter. Huppy took his ten deep breaths.

But like most puppies when they are frightened, he couldn't keep quiet. "What are we going to *do?*" he said.

# A Growing Dog

"The first thing we're going to do is not worry," said Harry. "But we *do* have to talk."

The time had come to discuss Huppy's future, and with the dog present, because it was *his* future, after all. Harry explained, as gently as he could, while Huppy's head hung down to his chest, that a cat and a mouse could live in a drainpipe, but—but—a growing dog couldn't. It wasn't that Tucker and he didn't want him there, or love him very much, it was just that it was—impossible. A dog needed space where he could live, and hopefully, a place to play. Harry said he'd been racking his brains for four months, and the only thing he'd been able to think of was—he looked away, down Forty-first Street, although Huppy hadn't lifted his eyes from the sidewalk—was for Huppy to go to Connecticut. The two of them would put him on the Late Local Express, at Grand Central Station.

"Where's Connecticut?" said Huppy.

Harry described Connecticut, where it was, how it looked, and began rhapsodizing about a beautiful, natural park up there, called the Old Meadow—"Renamed 'Tucker's Countryside,'" put in the mouse, "and for very good reason!"—and how they had this friend, Chester Cricket, who was very nice and could probably see that Huppy got adopted by a human family, and—

"I don't want to go to Connecticut!" said the dog.

"I don't blame you," sighed Tucker Mouse. "The country is a nice place to visit, but I wouldn't want to live there either."

"It sounds so far away," said Huppy. "Don't you even want to *visit* me?"

Tucker jumped up and tried to grab the dog's neck but fell back and had to content himself with hugging a foreleg. "Of course we want to visit you!"

"Besides," said Huppy, "I *like* New York!"

"There you are," said the mouse. "You're born in New York, you like New York—despite the mess it is. Despite the fact you've been thrown away in an alley on Tenth Avenue. Harry, this is a New York dog with a New York problem. We've got to solve it right here in New York. Leave Chester in peace."

"Then solve it!" said Harry, somewhat sulkily. "Well?"

"Well—" At the end of ten minutes of whisker wiggling, Tucker only came up with a meantime idea— until they could find Huppy a permanent home. He went over it with them. If Harry could get them back to the drainpipe that night—"Oh, I can. Once I've been through even the craziest labyrinth, I can find my way back again." And if Huppy would only not grow for one day—"I promise!" So Tucker outlined his meantime idea.

They all agreed it would have to do.

# A Growing Dog

The next night the plan was in effect. It was late, almost dawn, and the three animals were sitting in the very same doorway on Forty-first Street. Outside, the winter thaw still held, but inside them there was a dismal kind of chill. All day long, after certain arrangements were made, Tucker and Harry had been busy acting natural. And earlier that night there had been an especially tasty scrounged-up dinner—with unmelted ice cream for dessert—but no one would have called the atmosphere festive, despite all the small talk the cat and mouse made. Huppy had lapped his ice cream in silence. And in silence the three of them now were waiting.

Lulu Pigeon flapped down in front of them. "Okay, men," she said, "it's all set. Let's go."

"I need ten breaths of fresh air!" announced Huppy anxiously.

Harry gave the pigeon a private look, and said, "Go ahead, Huppy—help yourself."

Everybody pretended not to be counting, and the puppy took many more breaths than ten.

But soon Lulu Pigeon began to fidget. "We ought to get moving. Max said just before the sun came up. And Max isn't the kind of a guy you keep waiting."

"Come on." Harry nudged the dog with his shoulder. "And don't worry."

"I'm not!" insisted Huppy in a voice that broke off at the end in a squeak.

"Well, *I* am!" Tucker Mouse muttered to himself.

Tucker's plan was that since Lulu Pigeon had said dogs lived in Bryant Park, Huppy should stay down there—"temporarily, for a little while," he kept explaining to Huppy and Harry all day. (What Lulu had really said was a pack of dogs hung out in the park, but Tucker didn't like the sound of those words too well, so he left them out.) He'd sneaked down to the park that afternoon and talked it all over with the pigeon. She said jake by her but she'd have to ask Max —the gang leader. (Tucker didn't like that much either.)

They waited beside the stone basin of the winter-silenced fountain. Without anyone's knowing exactly when, a chunk of the darkness, which had also been waiting, took the shape of a dog and slipped up behind them. "This him?" came a muffled, deep voice.

"Gosh, you scared me!" squawked Lulu. The others had jumped up and turned around too.

"Quiet, bird."

Lulu flapped and said softly, "Yeah, Max—this is Huppy."

"Hi, kid." The voice seemed to be hiding a laugh somewhere.

Huppy hung his head down. "Hello." He couldn't see anything funny.

The pigeon introduced Tucker and Harry to Max. He was a gray dog, tough and much bigger than the cat. His eyes weren't round, like Huppy's eyes, beneath his fur; they were lifted a little—not slanted exactly, but questioning something: suspicious eyes. Ordinarily the animals in New York get along with each other fairly well, but Harry suspected that if he'd met Max on a prowl in the street he'd have gotten a snarl—maybe barking, and a fight. Not now, though. Lulu had explained everything, and Max just flicked his eyes disdainfully over both cat and mouse. "Come on, kid," he commanded Huppy softly. "Almost sunup. The cops'll be making their first rounds soon."

"Just like *that?*" burst out Tucker Mouse. "You take him away—"

"Sure, Tucker baby," said Max. "Just like that. You want me to show him the ropes, don't you?"

Tucker was about to launch into a string of orders —what he wanted, and didn't want, Max to do—but Harry shushed him and simply said, "We want you to take care of him. For a couple of days. Until we can find him a permanent home."

"Oh—a permanent home." Max laughed. "I've heard that before. And so has every other stray mutt in New York."

From the east a dull morning, lowering with clouds, inched toward the city. The wind had grown colder.

"Go on, Huppy," urged Harry Cat. "Go on with

Max. We'll be back tonight. To make sure you're all right."

"Goodbye," said Huppy.

They watched him shamble reluctantly off, and then run, to keep up with the lean and stealthy dog.

"I guess I'd better get going too," said Lulu.

"So go," muttered Tucker.

The cat and the mouse headed back to Times Square.

To put a dent in an iron silence Harry said, "I think the weather's going to change."

"The heck with the weather!" fumed Tucker Mouse. "What did you think of Max?"

"Well, I thought he looked—I mean, he looked—"

"He looked as if his father was a wolf and his mother was a weasel!" It didn't help Tucker one bit to remember that the whole thing had been his own idea.

And it didn't help either one of them to see Huppy's house when they got back home—empty.

"We aren't going to throw it out," declared Harry.

"You're darn right we're not!" It was loyalty, love— a pledge to Huppy—to keep it there, useless though it had become.

All morning long Tucker furiously rearranged his possessions. That was his way of trying to think. Harry's was just to sit in the drainpipe opening and watch— and not watch—the commotion go by; like having a background radio on but not bothering to listen to it.

Noon came, and the people who tramped down the

subway stairs were dusted with white: it was snowing outside.

"There he is again," said Harry.

"Who?" The mouse was holding a special prize: a red *unbroken* Christmas tree bauble, salvaged only a month ago.

"Mr. Smedley," said Harry.

"I don't know why he comes down here so often." Tucker couldn't decide where to relocate this latest treasure. "Sometimes he doesn't even buy a paper—just stands by the newsstand for hours, talking with Mama and Papa Bellini."

Mr. Smedley was the piano teacher who first—after Tucker—had discovered Chester Cricket's great gift. It was his letter to *The New York Times* that had made the cricket famous.

The mouse made up his mind: propped up on the high heel—the left rear corner—the ornament would look best. "He must be lonely."

"Lonely?"

"*Lonely!*" A crash! Red smithereens shimmered all over the drainpipe floor. Tucker didn't even notice them. He dashed up beside his friend. "Dumb me!"

"How stupid can an alley cat get! Right here, before our eyes—all this time."

They stared at the unsuspecting man, whose future seemed already leashed to him.

62

## A Growing Dog

"He's lonely, he's lonely," gloated Tucker Mouse in a singsong voice. He rubbed his claws together. "Now who can you think of to keep Mr. Smedley company?— and maybe take some piano lessons!"

FIVE

# Snow—and Other Complications

With the problem of Huppy—they thought—neatly solved, Tucker and Harry took the remainder of the afternoon off, for rest, relaxation, and self-congratulation. To be sure, a few details remained to be settled—such as how they could introduce Huppy to Mr. Smedley, and whether he would like the dog, much less want to adopt him—but in the first rush of relief, neither cat nor mouse could bother his head about such trivial practicalities. Besides, there was no chance to take any action today. Mr. Smedley stayed only for five or ten minutes, chatting with the Bellinis, who owned the newsstand—then he vanished downstairs to the IRT subway tracks. It definitely was a day for just lounging around, as snowy days often are, and for feeling the comfort and coziness of being indoors while it's storming outside.

And it really did snow! The animals could tell that because rush hour began an hour ahead of time. The people were let out of offices early to try to beat the weather home. By six o'clock the subway station was almost deserted, and those few human beings who straggled in looked like huffing and puffing snowmen.

But who cared?—in a drainpipe carpeted with clean newspapers, when all worries had been swept away. The only thing that nagged at the edges of Tucker's and Harry's pleasure was the thought of Huppy—out there in the blizzard somewhere. But they'd find out all about that tonight.

When Tucker's salvaged watch read ten, Harry said, "Come on—we promised."

"Don't need to tell me," declared Tucker Mouse.

They were both looking forward to the journey down to Bryant Park—because after being inside in a snowstorm, the next best thing is to be right out in the teeth of it. There was this pleasure also: one of the rare times that New York City looks really clean is when there's a blanket of snow over it. A fresh blanket, that is; in a couple of days New York snow turns sooty and dirty. (Another clean minute can come in the summer, just after a drenching rain. But that, too, does not last long.)

The cat and the mouse crept up through the pipes. But at their usual exit hole they were met with a hard blank wall of white.

Harry scratched at its surface. "Solid as concrete."

That could mean only one of two things: either there

was a howling wind outside that had packed the snow down this hard, or so much snow had fallen that the pedestrians had trampled it into a solid mass. In either case, it meant there would be no frolicking down an empty Forty-second Street, jumping in snowdrifts just for the fun of it.

In fact, it meant there was no going down Forty-second Street at all. After scratching his way a few feet, Harry's claws were in ruins. "No use," he said, "I can't make it. We'll have to wait till tomorrow."

"But Huppy—"

"Chances are, he and Max have holed up somewhere anyhow."

But the next day, a Friday, the blizzard continued. The cat and the mouse tried every single pipe route they knew, including the long way to Forty-first—with precisely the same result each time: no going out.

On Saturday morning the storm ended at last. The people in the subway station appeared without their white icing. But their teeth were chattering now. A cold spell had followed the snow. And since it was the weekend, nobody bothered to shovel out. The city lay frozen, glistening under the futile sun, still—as if bewitched by a sorcerer's winter spell.

The cold crept all the way down to the drainpipe. Tucker Mouse, who'd taken to sleeping in Huppy's house, shivered under four layers of newspapers.

Harry wrapped himself in the piece of red flannel shirt. "Those two dogs had *better* be holed up!" said Tucker. "Otherwise, they'll be frozen to death."

"They're holed up," Harry hoped.

"And what about Lulu? Why doesn't she fly over here and tell us what's happening?"

"She's probably down in that antique shop, buried under some moldy cushions right now."

"That kookoo bird," grumbled the mouse, and rubbed his ears to prevent frostbite.

By Monday—"I've had it!" shouted Tucker. In a flurry of ripped newspaper he jumped out of the card-

## Snow—and Other Complications

board box. "Let me out of here, Harry! I'm going stir-crazy!"

"I don't feel exactly like a June bug jumping around Central Park myself!" said Harry.

But it wasn't until Tuesday that the frigid enchantment was broken. The chill air seemed to breathe and come alive again. From the street above sounded gigantic scraping, as trucks with snowplows attached to their fronts did their final work. There was clanking, too, of iron chains: the last stalled snow-covered cars were being hauled away from the curb. The gutter would be clear tonight. In the afternoon a neater, nearer rustling told the animals that the sidewalk at last had been shoveled out. Their exit hole was free. Mama and Papa Bellini opened their newsstand in time for the evening rush, and most important—it seemed like fate to Harry Cat—Mr. Smedley dropped by to chat with them about the big blizzard.

"Okay—this is it," said the cat.

"This is what?"

"Tonight you go down to Bryant Park."

"*I* go down!" exclaimed Tucker. "And what, might I ask—"

"I'm following Mr. Smedley."

"What? What?" the mouse dithered. "We've got to have a plan."

"I'm *telling* you the plan," said Harry. "You go to the park—I'm pretty sure Huppy'll be there tonight, he must know how much we're worried about him—say hello, by the way, for me—and I'm shadowing Smedley. We've got to find out how the land lies, don't we?"

"But—but—"

"No buts!"

"—he may live in the Bronx."

"Then I'm going to the Bronx! Watch out—he's leaving. Have a good supper, Mousiekins. Stay here till most of the traffic dies down—and don't bother waiting up for me. I've got a feeling this may take a long time."

The cat chose his moment, then disappeared amidst hurrying, random feet.

Tucker Mouse got back from his travels at three o'clock the next morning. (To be exact, 3:05: the numbers on his watch were luminous and shed a nice glow at the back of the pipe.) His home was empty. Despite what Harry had said, the mouse decided that he would wait up. After what he'd seen and heard in the past three hours, sleep was out of the question now. And when Tucker waited, he really *waited*. He paced, he rearranged, he stared out angrily into the subway station. There are some poor people for whom waiting is harder work than working, and Tucker Mouse was such a one.

Occasionally he took time out from his waiting to fume. "Blood," he muttered to himself. "Hooligan!" His face pinched into a grimace as he mouthed two words: *"Tucker baby!"* Then he began to wait again, more intensely than before.

By that afternoon he was tired out and had to lie down. It didn't help. It only transferred all the useless activity inside his head.

He was so preoccupied—like a stretched rubber band, he lay on the papers in Huppy's house—that he didn't hear Harry Cat slip in. "I'm back."

"At *last!*"

"Who first?"

"You first."

"Okay," said Harry. "I almost lost Smedley on the IRT platform, but I found him and followed."

*"Just wait till you hear what's happened to Huppy!"*

"All right," sighed the cat. "You first."

*"Well—"* Tucker's story burst out of him. "I waited till midnight, then went down to the park, a forlorn and lonely figure, creeping his way through ice and snow—"

"Just skip the poetry and get to the point."

"—a forlorn and lonely figure!" Tucker glared at his friend. A day's waiting, he thought, entitled him to tell it his way. "And what do I find in Bryant Park? A pack of dogs going sliding! You know, at the back of the park is the New York Public Library. The wind blew a big drift up against it, and the sun today melted just enough snow to make ice tonight—and there were all these dogs going sliding! And you know what they

were sliding on?" The mouse paused dramatically. "Their bottoms!"

"I didn't *think* they had toboggans," said Harry.

Tucker ignored the dig. "So up I marched, very fearlessly, expecting that I would be chewed up. Which I almost was!—by those hoodlum mutts. Excuse the word, but that's what they were. They mauled me something awful, till the head hooligan—that's Max!— came sliding down on his fanny and said, 'Lay off the rodent.' Meaning *me*—Tucker Mouse!"

In a fit of outrage Tucker became completely tongue-tied. Harry waited patiently till he'd spluttered himself into mere indigation. "For the rest of the time I was down there he called me 'Tucker baby,' too!"

"Insult to injury," murmured the cat. "But what about Huppy?"

"Oh, he came sliding down, too—and knocked me flat on my back, he did. That made Lulu Pigeon— she was up in a tree, enjoying my discomfiture—laugh even louder. '*Oo! oo! oo!*'—you know how that kookoo bird laughs."

"Get on with the story!" said Harry Cat, whose patience, about now, was running out.

"All right, all right. So Huppy knocks me down, I get up, and—oh, Harry, he's grown! He's huge! In less than a week he's almost twice his size. No wonder, with what he's been eating. So after I get up, the first thing I notice, besides his size, is this stain on the whiskers around his mouth. I say, 'Huppy, what is that stain around your mouth?' He licks at it and says, 'Oh, that's just blood.' "

"*Blood!*"

"Exactly what I meant to say myself—'Blood!'—but before I could scream my anguish out, Huppy says, 'Come on, Tucker baby.' He too, by the way, is now calling me 'Tucker baby'!—'come on, Tucker baby! Take a slide yourself!' And before I knew what was happening, he had grabbed the back of my neck in his teeth, dragged me up to the top of this mountainous drift, sat me down, pushed me off. And Harry, I have to admit—*hic! hic! hic!*" Tucker squeaked his raspy little laugh. "It's quite a lot of fun! I had four slides and nearly wore off all my fur you-know-where. You should try it yourself some—"

"I'm going to *clobber* you!"

"O-*kay!* So I had four slides and then I said, 'Huppy, enough of this childishness. What blood?' 'From the butcher shop!' he happily announced, and launched himself down the slope again. You see, Harrykins, we needn't have wasted our worry on Huppy. While we were down here in this drainpipe freezing our noses off, little Huppy was off carousing with Max and the other mutts. And *I*, Tucker Mouse, am here to tell *you*, Harry Cat, that Max knows this city even better than you do! They spent the blizzard in the toasty-warm cellar of an office building on Madison Avenue. Because Max knows *all* the buildings with sleepy night watchmen who sometimes leave the door unlocked or with watchmen frightened of snarling dogs—"

"Huppy snarls?"

"He's learning fast!" said Tucker. "He gave me a very convincing snarl, to show. Just give him a couple weeks more, he'll have added growling, barking, howling, all kinds of lovely doggy things to his repertory."

"I don't like that." Harry shook his head.

"You'll like what comes next even less. Just listen. The storm being over, Max leads the pack to the Upper East Side, where, on Lexington Avenue now, is located an especially expensive butcher shop—with a conveniently broken back window! Friend Max is also an expert on broken windows, broken doors, broken anything, where a dog can get in. And if nothing is broken, they've even got a big part-Saint Bernard named Louie—very small in the brains, however—whose specialty is rearing up on his hind legs and pressing down on door handles. At Max's direction, of course. So anyway, for two whole days the dogs gorged themselves on top round ground, lamb chops, and prime rib roasts." Tucker licked his lips at the thought of it all. "Which, despite how delicious the meat may have been, and despite that the place where they put the treasure was their own bulging bellies—is what you'd call stealing."

"You've been known to pilfer from the lunch stand yourself."

Tucker glared at the cat. "And since when did *you* turn down—"

"Oh, forget it." Harry flicked his tail around his forelegs impatiently. "Is that all?"

"That is *not* all. All came at the end of my visit to dogsville. I managed to drag Huppy off to one side and talk to him privately. And I told him we'd found a place for him."

"Did you tell him where?" Harry interrupted.

"I don't *know* where yet. That was up to you. Why?"

"You'll see. Go on."

"So I told him we'd probably found him a home, and *he* said that what with the tasty raw meat he'd been eating and what with the fun of sliding down snowdrifts, he wasn't at all sure he wanted to split from the gang! His very words: 'split from the gang.' "

"All right. I get it."

"So that is my story," concluded Tucker. "We've got to hurry! Now what is yours?"

"Sit down," said the cat. "You're in for a shock."

# SIX

# Miss Catherine

"He lives way uptown," began Harry, "on the West Side, in the Sixties. It wasn't too hard to follow him. I rode between the cars on the subway, away from the human beings, but where I could see him when he got off. The first problem came when we got to the apartment house."

"In a slum?" guessed Tucker.

"Just the opposite. A nice street—big old buildings —and Mr. Smedley's apartment house is the best on the block."

"No pets?" Tucker guessed again.

Harry shook his head. "A man went in ahead of Mr. Smedley with an Afghan hound on a leash."

"And they're big!" the mouse chortled gleefully. "Even bigger than Huppy'll probably get. So what was the problem?"

"The problem was me. Afghans on leashes, yes— stray alley cats, no. The doorman shooed me away."

"The snob!"

"I sat across the street and watched Mr. Smedley go into the lobby, then into the elevator—the doors closed —he was gone. And somewhere, I thought, inside that building there might be a home for Huppy. But it was at least twenty stories tall. So what was I to do?"

"Claw the doorman, and while he's running away you read Mr. Smedley's apartment number on the mailboxes, then find the emergency staircase and—"

"I promise not to ask any more rhetorical questions, if you promise to shut up," said Harry.

"Okay," sulked Tucker, who still liked his plan. "What *did* you do?"

"I decided the place for an alley cat was an alley. So I sneaked through the one beside the building, and in back of it I found what I was looking for: a fire escape."

"That's the boy!" burst in Tucker enthusiastically. "That Max may think he knows the ins and outs of the city, but he can't beat Harry Cat! Go, man!"

"I went," said Harry. "First onto the top of a trash can, then, with a big jump, all the way up to the very last rung of the ladder at the bottom of the fire escape. And a long trip began. I didn't mind the fire escape— they're great for cats—but where was Mr. Smedley? And how was I going to get in? The escape was on the hall of each floor, and the window into the hall was not only shut but locked."

"Well? *Well?*"

"I was counting on luck," the cat continued. "Cats *do* have luck."

"A little should rub off on me," Tucker muttered.

"And when I'm out prowling on an adventure like this I have found I can count on at least one good-sized chunk of luck. And I got it! On the seventeenth floor. I crept up all those metal stairs, and then I heard it— piano playing! That wasn't the luck, though. Anybody could have heard the piano playing. The luck was, the window into the hall was broken. One pane of glass was completely out. In I jumped and listened my way to Apartment G. That's where the sound was coming from. 'Course, there might have been other human beings with pianos in that apartment house—but this *had* to be Mr. Smedley! I recognized the piece he was playing. It was one of those things Chester Cricket played when he gave his concerts over at the newsstand. And it *sounded* like Mr. Smedley, too. Kind of finicky and nervous, but nice. So the next problem was how to get in."

"More luck?"

"No. Only frustration. I sat in that hall for an hour, just wondering what to do. I'd about decided to start miaowing pitifully and pretend I had a broken leg— then he'd open the door to see what all the racket was —but it didn't come to that. The piano playing stopped, and I heard him say, 'Ah, lovely! Such a charming piece!' "

"That's great!" laughed Tucker. "The guy talks to himself. He must *really* be lonely."

"Just hold your horses," warned Harry Cat. " 'Lovely, lovely,' he said. I heard him walk from one room to another, the sound of dishes rattling—he was in the kitchen, making supper. The refrigerator door opened. 'Oh, drat!' he said. 'No milk. Well, we have to have milk.' Now a rustling sound, right inside the door—he was putting on his overcoat. And I knew in an instant what to do. I flattened myself against the floor, squinched up against the wall, and as soon as that apartment door opened, I was in like a flash—before he could even look down."

"Whoopee!" shouted Tucker. "Alone in Mr. Smedley's apartment! A perfect chance to case the joint. As Max would say. What's it like?"

"Beautiful—in a kind of old-fashioned way. He'd left the light on in the hall, and with that, plus my cat's eyes, I got a good look at everything. I could tell right away that Mr. Smedley must come from a long line of somebodies or other. Almost every stick of furniture in the place is antique. And *good* antiques, too! I've prowled through enough antique shops in the city to recognize quality when I see it. Except in Mr. Smedley's apartment there may be too many of them."

"But how many rooms?" interrupted Tucker.

"Well—" Harry counted on his paws. "The kitchen, the dining room, living room, the music room, Mr.

Smedley's bedroom—he has a big brass bedstead—the guest bedroom, those rooms at the back—at least eight or nine, I guess."

"Eight or nine!" Tucker rubbed his claws together in glee. "That means Huppy can have one all to himself. We could maybe even set up a little summer place for ourselves."

"The most interesting one is the music room. There's a big piano there, a grand, and a second, littler one. I guess for teaching he sometimes plays along with his students. And the walls are lined with bookshelves full of books of music and opera librettos—and records. The one new thing in the whole apartment is a beautiful hi-fi set, with four speakers. But even there—"

"What even there?" Tucker heard the change come in Harry's voice, as the cat stopped to think.

"I mean, even with the hi-fi set there's a feeling of oldness. I don't mean oldness—I like old things—but mustiness. And a sicklish sweetness in the air. It's especially strong in the living room. Not dust or dirt—everything's all clean—but you *know* that the sofa has not been moved for years. And the glass candlesticks on the mantelpiece—they have *got* to be in exactly the spot where Mr. Smedley's mother left them."

"Fresh air!" diagnosed Tucker Mouse. "That's all Mr. Smedley needs. And fresh life." He poked his friend in the ribs. "That's something that we can provide—eh, Harry?"

"Fresh life," mused Harry. "I was thinking something like that myself as I looked all around that crowded living room. Then I heard it."

"Heard what?"

"A voice." Harry paused—not to tease, but reliving the eerie memory.

"Harry—if you wouldn't drive me crazy, please. Talk!"

"A voice." Harry shook himself into the present. "From somewhere above me. It said, 'Well, sir—and now that you've seen everything, might I ask what it is that you mean to steal?' "

"A ghost!" exclaimed Tucker. "The apartment is haunted!"

"It's haunted, all right. But not by the kind of ghost you think. I looked up, where the voice was coming from. Against one wall there's this secretary. That's a big old elaborate desk with a bookcase built on top of it, and glass doors to the bookcase. The top shelf of this particular secretary was full of china animals. There were birds, a monkey, a china collie—and a life-size china Siamese cat. Which was *not* made of china! In the dim light filtering in from the hall I saw the cat's eyes slowly close and open."

"Oh, my gosh—"

"Oh, my gosh is right, Mousiekins. Mr. Smedley already *has* a pet—and her name is Miss Catherine. It was her that he was talking to, not himself. And it also was from her—I found out when she jumped down beside me—that that weak sweet smell in the air came from. Mr. Smedley puts a drop of perfume on her every now and then."

"*Per*-fume!" gasped Tucker.

"To the desk, to the floor, right beside me she jumped. And repeated, 'Well?' in an outraged voice. 'If there's nothing to satisfy a thief here, there's some silver in the dining room!' "

"Harry—I wouldn't want to interrupt—but you didn't happen to take maybe a spoon—"

"I did *not* take a spoon!" Harry angrily said. "Or

anything else. Since my mind, right then, wasn't on your collection!"

"Too bad. But okay."

"I assured her that I was not a thief, and so naturally she demanded what I *was* doing there, in that case. And I told her."

"The truth?"

"The whole truth. And don't make it sound like a red-hot iron. Sooner or later it would have to come out. I told her everything about Huppy—finding him, losing him, finding him again, his growing so fast—the works, ending up with Mr. Smedley being our only hope."

"You told her about me, too?" said Tucker. "What did she say?"

"She said, 'Hmm!' and sniffed."

"Well, I say, 'Hmm!' and sniff right back!"

"When I got to the part about Huppy living up there, she looked at me as if I was crazy. 'What?' she said, aghast. 'A *dog?* Residing here? With me and Horatio? It simply won't do!' She was going to go on, but just then Horatio himself got back with the milk. Miss Catherine said that if I wished 'to pursue this nonsense,' I should hide in the music room while they had dinner. Mr. Smedley always goes to bed early. And when he *had* gone to bed, and she and I were pursuing the nonsense, I found out that she is thirteen years old."

"That's old for a cat, isn't it?" asked Tucker.

# Miss Catherine

"Pretty old," admitted Harry, "but she's got grit. After all, I could really have been a burglar and beaten her up." He paused. "On the other paw, I think she might have won a cat fight at that. Anyway, she's thirteen, she belonged to Mr. Smedley's mother, she likes her drop of perfume now and then—but she also likes to go out for an outing, even on winter afternoons. That's rare, because Siamese cats hate the cold. He takes her to Riverside Park. All that I found out after dinner. During dinner I found out something much more important. Mr. Smedley is not in charge of his own apartment. Miss Catherine Cat is! She's got the guy wrapped around one ear. You should have heard him. 'Would Miss Catherine like—' "

"Wait a minute," said Tucker. "She refers to him as Horatio and he calls her *Miss* Catherine?"

"That's the kind of cat she is," said Harry. "But sometimes, in a gush of love, he also calls her Puss-puss."

"*Puss*-puss!"

" 'Does Puss-puss crave more lovely cube steak? Does Puss-puss thirst for a bit more milk?' "

"*Yich!*" Tucker Mouse grimaced disgust. "Sickmaking! That's one guy who really needs a dog."

"Sick-making or not, them's the facts."

"Enough of facts! When does Huppy move up?"

"Are you crazy!" shouted Harry. "Haven't you heard a word I've said? She will not hear of it! I wheedled her all last night, and I wheedled her all today while Mr.

Smedley and some very untalented little boys banged away at those pianos—and all I got was permission to come back again and talk. Pursue the nonsense! An hour ago she showed me the back door to 'my apartment.' The door didn't close completely, and the two of us managed to pry it open. 'The servants' entrance,' she explained. 'In future please use this. I believe in the basement you'll find a window ajar. Good day.' "

"That's how she says goodbye?"

"That's how she doesn't say goodbye."

Tucker sat a minute silently, except for some growling—which sounded, in his case, more like a squeak beneath the breath. "Well—I'm not sure I want Huppy living there anyway."

"You have any better ideas?"

Tucker didn't. "This is great!" he said. "This is really great. On the one paw we have Max, with his pack of four-legged gangsters, and on the other, two old maids—Horatio Smedley and Catherine Cat."

"*Miss* Catherine," Harry sweetly corrected him.

# SEVEN

# Pursuing the Nonsense

A few weeks later Tucker Mouse was fuming, furious, and fit to be tied—a not unusual state for him these days. He was alone—he was almost always alone now—sitting in the deserted drainpipe, trying to patch up a paper flower with a bit of Scotch tape. Both flower and tape had been salvaged that very afternoon from the treasure trove that an overflowing trash basket can be.

"It's humiliating," the mouse mumbled. (Among other strange practices like mending paper flowers, he had taken to talking to himself. Nowadays, it seemed to him, there was nobody else to talk to.) "Degrading!—that's what it is." The Scotch tape got stuck to the fur on his chest. "The worst time in my life." He yanked off the tape. Some fur came with it.

The worst time in Tucker Mouse's life began the day after Harry had made the acquaintance of Miss Catherine. He slept late the next morning, and when he woke up, after having a bite to eat—from Tucker's carefully hoarded food—he decided that he would visit her, take her up right away on her invitation. "Strike while the iron's hot," he said.

"So go strike," said Tucker.

But on the way out Harry saw something new. "What's that?"

"*That*," the mouse proclaimed proudly, "is a piece of carefully rolled-up pink ribbon. Rescued this morning from the Loft's Candy Shop. A salesgirl was wrapping up a box as a gift, and—"

"I'm taking it," Harry announced.

"You're *what?*"

"When you visit, you're supposed to bring a gift."

"Well, get your own gift!" said Tucker. "She's *your* friend."

"No time." He scooped up the neat roll with one paw. "Besides, I've got a feeling that she'll like this." Then he thought better of it and popped the bundle into his mouth. That way he could carry it carefully and not get it dirty. Before the mouse could begin to moan, he was gone.

And that night, when he got back, there sat Tucker gloomily in the absence of his pretty pink ribbon. "I was right. She liked it."

"Why shouldn't she like it?" demanded Tucker. "I would have you to understand, precious things like that don't grow on trees. No wonder she thought you were a thief."

Harry ignored the fancy language—a sure sign of a mouse's displeasure—as well as the dig, and said, "She's got a hope chest."

"What's a hope chest?"

"It's a kind of an old-fashioned habit." Harry smiled. "And it's nice. A place where single ladies—lady cats, lady dogs, lady human beings—keep things that they like. And they hope."

"So? What do they hope for?"

"What *would* they?"

"For an old bag like Miss Catherine—"

"She's not an old bag! She's a middle-aged cat."

"—it's too late," finished Tucker.

"I don't care," said Harry. The same smile flickered. "I think it's nice. Miss Catherine's hope chest is the sewing basket of Mr. Smedley's mother. That's where she put the ribbon, along with her other favorite things. She told me all about them over a bowl of milk we shared."

While Tucker grumbled on jealously—he was only jealous about the milk, of course, since he would have liked a sip himself—Harry Cat was getting some good ideas, which he wisely decided to keep to himself. The first was, how alike Miss Catherine and Tucker were in their passion for collecting things. The second—they had similar tastes, too: a fondness for buckles and beads and bright whatnots, although sometimes Tucker lost his head over crazy things like high heels. And the *third* idea was—!

"Now about this bead," said the cat next morning.

"What about my *favorite green bead?*" Tucker snatched back his jewel. (It was only glass, but an emerald couldn't have been more precious.)

"Well, I was just thinking—"

"I know what you're thinking! You know what I'm thinking? Let her get out and scrounge for herself! I'm not about to donate my collection to an old maid's hope chest!"

"All right," sighed Harry and looked away. A sad, distant expression came into his eyes. "I wonder if Huppy's learned to pick locks yet."

A heavy minute passed. Then, "Take the bead," said Tucker hopelessly. A terrible feeling of defeat overcame him. And the worst of it was, he felt that his misery was just beginning.

He was right. The cat's requests began with a ribbon, went on through beads, and were only brought to a screeching halt when he asked for a dime. *"No!"* shouted Tucker. "No loose change does she get! Not over my dead body!" Harry let the matter drop. He knew when a mouse had reached his limits. (But he still went on asking for—begging, if necessary, and grudgingly getting—some of Tucker's most choice possessions.)

In desperation the mouse took to ransacking all the trash baskets in the Times Square subway station while Harry was out. He found that most days he was able to dredge up satisfactory substitutes for his priceless junk. Such valuables as a pair of glasses with one lens still in, an automatic pencil *with* leads—to give that up almost broke his heart—and on this particular afternoon a ripped and laboriously repaired paper flower.

"There!" he said to the flower angrily. "And I hope she notices the fur under the Scotch tape."

There was a whoosh of braking wings at the drainpipe opening and Lulu Pigeon waddled in. "Ooo, Tucker, that's *darling!*" she said. "Who's it for?"

"The Empress of the Upper West Side!" snapped the mouse. "As if you didn't know."

"*Oo! oo! oo!*" the pigeon gargled her falsetto laugh.

"And please, Lulu, you wouldn't make fun of another soul's unhappiness."

Since he was alone so much lately, Tucker had gotten into the habit of complaining to Lulu about the sorrows of the world—and his own in particular. She wasn't exactly the most serious confidante he could think of, but in this pinch, he found, she would do. Any reasonably sympathetic ear was a help.

"Harry up paying court?" she asked.

"He is *not* paying court!" announced the mouse firmly. "I have told you repeatedly he is up there trying to con Miss Catherine into letting Huppy go live in Mr. Smedley's apartment."

The reason Tucker was seeing so much of Lulu Pigeon was that, what with his recent pressing duties, he didn't have time to go down to Bryant Park every night. So Lulu came to him, with bulletins about the dog. And the bulletins were mostly bad, so bad that Tucker began to think of his friend as a bird of ill omen—a kookoo bird of ill omen, at that.

"How *is* Huppy, by the way?" he asked. "Did you tell him to take a bath, like I said?—but to stay somewhere warm till his fur dries out so he wouldn't catch—"

"I told him everything."

"Did he do it?"

"No. He said, 'Phooey!' and went off with the pack." Tucker shook his head. "He must be a mess."

"He's beautiful!" said Lulu. "Just the color of soot. He blends right in to the city snow. The cops'll never catch that dog."

"Lulu—thank you for all this cheery information, but if you're in a hurry—"

"I'm not in a hurry. Besides, I want to say hello to— and speak of the devil! Here he is! Hi, Harry."

"Hi, Lulu." Harry Cat slipped into the drainpipe, and as usual the first thing he did was to lick himself clean. The trip uptown and back was very messy these winter days, and like the people who live in New York the cats there either stay especially clean or else tend to turn into bums.

"How's tricks, man?"

"Not so hot, Lulu. Some kids spraying graffiti on the subway cars decided that it would be lots more fun to spray me. And while I was running away from them, a lady wearing boots stepped right on my tail. It wasn't her fault, though—she didn't see me."

"Enough with the tail! The tail will get better. How did Miss Catherine like the two plastic toothpicks I sent up yesterday?"

"Not much. And that's something we've got to talk about, all that stuff. When Miss Catherine saw the toothpicks, she just laughed and said, 'Really, Harry—' "

"Since when does she call you Harry?"

"Oh, she's called me by my first name for days."

"Very charming," nodded Tucker. "In another year or two she may call you Puss-puss."

"What's wrong with you?" The cat recognized a certain perilous edge in his friend's voice.

"There's nothing wrong with me! I'll tell you what's wrong with me! I am sick, Harry Cat, sick and tired of working my claws to the bone for the sake of a pampered—"

"Now hold on, Tucker—"

"—a pampered house cat! And speaking of working my claws to the bone, and having my fur torn out—"

"*Were* we speaking of having your fur torn?" purred Harry impatiently. His fur began to rise and crackle with electricity.

"Yes!" Tucker shouted. "Here's a present for Puss-puss for tomorrow!" He threw the patched flower straight in Harry's face.

"That flower?"

"That flower! What's wrong with that flower?"

"A pack rat wouldn't have dragged it home."

"Are you calling me a rat?"

"*Oo! oo! oo!*" Lulu Pigeon wasn't exactly a bad bird, but she had a mischievous sense of humor and didn't mind getting a few good laughs out of watching friends quarrel.

"I'm not calling you a pack rat," hissed Harry through his teeth. "I'm just saying this gift is absurd!"

"Absurd!" It was as if someone had pulled Tucker's whisker of self-respect. "I will not be made to look absurd." He ripped up the flower furiously. "And I've had it, Harry! I've had it up to here!" He held his claw beneath his chin—not too high, perhaps, but for an outraged mouse, the limit. "Why don't you go up and *live* with Miss Catherine? Just jump in her hope chest— she can keep you there with the rest of the junk! Since you don't like this pack rat's home." He crumpled the torn pieces into a ball. "And when you get up there,

give *this* to Miss Catherine, with my love!" And threw it straight into Harry's face.

"All right, that did it!" Harry stood on his four legs, trembling, and advanced on Tucker threateningly. For an instant they seemed like nothing but natural enemies—cat, mouse—and blood was in the few inches of air that separated the two of them.

"Okay, boys—break it up!" Lulu Pigeon waddled between them and spread her wings apart. "Enough's enough. Who would have thought anybody could bust up the happiest drainpipe in all New York? Harry Cat and Tucker Mouse—" She clucked her tongue reprovingly. "Tsk, tsk, tsk."

Harry and Tucker looked away from each other. Eyes, when you're ashamed, can be painful.

"Now shake hands," ordered Lulu. "Or shake paws. Shake claws. Shake anything!"

They shook.

"It's my nerves," explained Tucker. "I'm worried—about Huppy."

"My tail," explained Harry.

"You want some ice? I could get some ice for your tail from the lunch stand."

"No, thanks. It'll be all right."

And making friends again, after anger, then shame, is a pleasure that starts hard, but ends with a special ease.

"It's so stupid to fight," said Harry Cat. "Today especially. I have good news."

Tucker's hope leaped into his mouth. "Will she *take* him?"

"She's consented to an interview."

"An interview—"

"That's all. For now."

Tucker tried to swallow his hope again.

"Well? Where do we meet?" said Lulu.

"We?" said Harry.

"*We?*" said Tucker.

"Why, sure!" cooed the pigeon. "You don't think I'd miss this, do you? *Oo! oo! oo!*"

# EIGHT

# Festivities

"I *am* absurd," sighed Tucker hopelessly, as he took a break from his labors in the kitchen quarter of the drainpipe. "I act absurd, I feel absurd." He glanced into a piece of broken mirror propped against one wall. "I look absurd—I'm absurd!" It was very little consolation, but he popped a sliver of ham in his mouth. Stealing tidbits in advance is allowed to a cook, and Tucker felt he deserved a treat.

It's a very good thing that he and Harry had had their almost-fight two days before, because if they hadn't, the mouse would certainly have been spoiling for it tonight. When Harry had said that Miss Catherine would permit an interview, what he hadn't let on, right away, was that she had added, in a petulant voice, that she "certainly would *not* allow the animal in Horatio's apartment." She would come down to Bryant Park herself. And Harry had also failed to tell Tucker, until he thought the mouse could take it, that he had been so impressed by Miss Catherine's offer, well, he'd asked her to stop by the drainpipe on her way down, for a bite to eat. Hence Tucker's resigned absurdity. For even he had to admit there was something truly ludicrous about a mouse preparing a dinner party for two cats—with a crazy bird thrown in!

Lulu Pigeon was the first guest to arrive. "Hi, man!"

"Hi, Lulu." Tucker munched his ham gloomily.

"Harry up collecting the guest of honor?"

"Not 'collecting,' Lulu." Tucker daintily lifted one claw. "He's 'escorting' her down to my humble home."

"Groovy!" said Lulu. "This is going to be a classy bash, I see."

"I got a feeling I'm the one who's getting bashed," said Tucker.

"Oh, boy—bread crumbs!" The pigeon waddled toward a succulent heap that Tucker had piled up for her earlier in the evening. "And *raisin* bread crumbs— wow! You're really putting on the dog."

"Get your beak out of those bread crumbs, Lulu! Nobody eats till everyone's here."

"You're eating—"

"I need it." Tucker swallowed. "And that was the last until Madame Queen makes her entry."

Like most good hosts, Tucker couldn't relax while he waited for his party to start. He fidgeted around the part of the floor that he had decided was a dining-room table, rearranging ripped but clean paper napkins, making sure that each animal's own special Dixie cup was placed just so, and generally making himself and Lulu Pigeon so nervous that she was about to tell him to cool it—when, with a swish of fur against pipe, the two cats appeared.

"Miss Catherine," Harry began the introductions, "this is Tucker, Tucker Mouse, my friend, and this is Lulu, Lulu Pigeon, a friend of the family, you might say. Ha, ha." Harry was fairly nervous himself—his laugh broke apart—since he was very well aware how much depended upon tonight.

"I've heard much about you, Mr. Mouse," said Miss Catherine.

Tucker had promised himself that he wouldn't be intimidated by his guest. But he was. She was truly an elegant, aristocratic feline, with her sleek beige Siamese fur and her chocolate-brown head, which she held a little bit aloof. Her eyes were china blue, and more than most cats' eyes—much more than Harry's—they felt as if they went right through Tucker's own little black beads. Also, to the mouse's amazement, she'd come all the way down from the Upper West Side without even smudging herself—quite a trick for what he had thought a spoiled house cat.

He stuttered a moment, then managed to say, "Yeah —well—I'm glad you could make it, Miss Catherine."

"Miss Pigeon—" With a very slight nod of her head, Miss Catherine acknowledged Lulu's presence.

"Hiya, Kate!" cooed the kookoo bird.

Harry and Tucker glanced frantically at one another. Had the black slit in her Siamese eyes become even narrower?

But if she was offended at Lulu Pigeon's impertinence, Miss Catherine never let on. She was too well brought up for that. Her gaze slid impassively over Tucker's and Harry's faces, as if they were only two more objects, like the high heel or the broken mirror. "So this is the famous drainpipe, is it? Mmmm," she purred. "Most interesting."

"Uh—if you'd like, Miss Catherine"—Tucker sounded as little like a mouse and as much like a gallant Afghan hound as he could—"I could show you around."

"Hey, you guys, let's chow down! My stomach's rumbling!"

It's a well-known fact—known only to themselves, perhaps—that animals with fur can blush like mad beneath their hair.

Harry hid his embarrassment by making small talk, which he did very well, but not nearly as well as Miss Catherine. Being Siamese, and so naturally talkative, but even more so because of her perfect training, she knew how to make the simplest things seem absolutely fascinating. She and Harry exchanged observations on the food, the napkins—since it was just small talk, they didn't have to believe each other—on everything and anything. Anything, that is, to drown out Lulu.

She did need some drowning out too, because she, at least, was one person who thought she knew what a dinner party was all about. It was all about dinner!—not talk. She waded into her food—quite literally: she walked right into the pile of bread crumbs—with relish, and her bill began to snap. Its clacking was only silenced when she stopped long enough—"Ooooo!"—to moan with pleasure at finding a crumb with melted butter soaked into it.

Needless to say, unlike the pigeon's, Miss Catherine's manners were beautiful. As well as being able to travel twenty blocks on a winter night and not get dirty, she was also the only cat that Tucker Mouse had ever seen who could lap up milk without making a sound.

As for Tucker, he was his usual self—a bundle of scurrying furry nerves. He ran back and forth between his pantry, which was only a pantry because that was where the food was stored before being served, and the dining-room table, and got so preoccupied in making sure that Miss Catherine had enough to eat that he almost forgot to eat himself. But not quite.

On several of these trips he stopped, accidentally, beside Lulu Pigeon and, when no one was looking, gouged her in the ribs, by way of advising her to eat more quietly. When she'd had enough of that—four gouges—she interrupted her munching, said, "What's with the elbow, Mickey Mouse?" and whacked him with a wing. It sent him sprawling. He could only grin

up from the floor at Harry and Miss Catherine and pretend that nothing at all had happened.

Dessert was the mouse's usual special: unmelted ice cream. The night before, Tucker had rescued a very large chunk—almost a whole scoop—of vanilla from the counter of the lunch stand. He had an elaborate way, which only worked in the winter, of keeping it solid. He would pack the ice cream in a paper cup and then drag it up through all the pipes, away from the warmth of the subway station, almost to the sidewalk. And then pray that the weather stayed below freezing. Last night, since he wanted it to be a surprise, he had done all the work of dragging alone while Harry was asleep. Quite a trick, the whole procedure was, if Tucker had to say so himself.

And he thought he *would* have to say so himself—until Miss Catherine, in between her ladylike licks, purred, "Most delicious, Mr. Mouse." A grin began to stretch Tucker's whiskers. "Of course my favorite flavor—Horatio's, too—is butter pecan. But, really, this is very nice."

"Thank you," said the mouse morosely.

"My favorite flavor's vanilla," said Lulu Pigeon. She was using the lower half of her beak as a scoop to dish up the lovely ice cream. When she'd finished her portion, a hiccup—which may have been something a little more impolite—resounded through the drainpipe. It was not concealed by the rapid conversation that Tucker and Harry and Miss Catherine made.

With two delicate swipes of her tongue, Miss Catherine licked her whiskers clean. "Yes, I must admit"—she nodded her head graciously toward Tucker—"a *most* satisfactory meal!"

"Oh, we eat like this all the time," he answered her airily.

"*Oo! oo! oo!*"

"Shut up, Lulu," Tucker warned the pigeon beneath his breath. He'd worked like a beaver to bring this dinner party off, and impress Miss Catherine favorably, and he wasn't about to put up with any of Lulu's sarcasm now.

"I believe," the Siamese said condescendingly, "that before I meet the animal we ought to discuss—"

"Miss Catherine!" That was too much for Tucker—good impression or not. "Please! You wouldn't call him an 'animal.' He's a *dog*—a very nice little dog, called Huppy."

"So Harry has told me," replied Miss Catherine with dry ice in her voice. "A little dog who's so nice you're afraid he's becoming a criminal."

"Well, I wouldn't go so far as to say that—" began Tucker.

"*I* would!" Harry Cat finished it for him. "She's right. Face facts. Huppy's going to the dogs."

"*Oo! oo! oo!*"

"*Now* what's so hilarious?" demanded Tucker.

"Huppy's going to the dogs," said the pigeon. "Where else would a puppy go?"

"That isn't funny!" shouted the mouse. "Lulu—just keep quiet, please. Since this doesn't concern you."

"Sure it does!" She flapped her wings grandly. "I love Huppy too!"

"One wonders," purred Miss Catherine, smooth as silk now, "why there should be any problem at all. When the dog has such splendid, intelligent friends."

The pigeon was too good-natured—her enemies

would have said stupid, if she'd had any—to understand a cat's wisecrack, even when it was aimed at her. "There *is* no problem! Just leave him be. Max is grooming him swell. He's already his sidekick. May even take over the pack some day. Be a really top dog in New York!"

"What more could one ask?" smirked Miss Catherine, with a sidelong glance at Harry.

He wasn't laughing with her, however. He avoided her eyes, as much for her own sake as anyone else's—that she should behave this way. And Tucker was not amused at all. A frown wrinkled his face. He distrusted most cats—except Harry—and especially distrusted a cat being catty.

But blissful Lulu plunged right on, unaware of the tension building around her. "You guys should see Max and Huppy together! He's teaching the kid to fight."

"Fight?" said Harry. This was an unwelcome development. "Since when?"

"Since this afternoon, just before I left. Sicked him onto big dumb Louie, Max did. Oo! oo! oo! The funniest thing I ever saw!"

"I'm sure it was charming," cooed Miss Catherine without so much as a flicker of an eyelid to suggest she was mimicking Lulu.

"There was the little guy, hanging onto the big guy's—hey, are you making fun of me, sister?"

"I wouldn't *dream* of it!"

" 'Cause if you are—"

Harry Cat stepped forward. "I think maybe we ought to go down to the park right now."

"That's a *grand* idea!" Tucker seconded him enthusiastically. He was beginning to think there was something about the Huppy problem that brought out the worst in everyone and made all New York animals want to fight with each other. "The sooner we can get him up to Miss Catherine's apartment—"

"There's no *question* of that!" said Miss Catherine firmly. "A great clumsy dog?—in *our* apartment? Ridiculous!—with all our lovely things all around. It won't do. Why, Horatio and I—we'd feel absurd—"

"Welcome to the club," mumbled Tucker.

Luckily, Miss Catherine didn't hear. She was too busy exclaiming about the idiocy of the whole idea. "But in the basement of the apartment house—we'll see. At least several weeks, I should think. And then, if I'm able to train him, perhaps for an hour or two each day, in one of the rear rooms—"

"Are you going to let this hunk of fluff take our Huppy uptown?"

"Are you referring to *me*, Miss Pigeon?"

"No, dear, I'm referring to my right eyeball." Lulu turned back to Harry and Tucker. "*Are* you? Ol' Puss-in-Boots'll just turn him into a prissy puppy—"

"Harry! I insist that you make this feathered thing stop calling me names!"

"Honey, this feathered thing"—Lulu hitched up her chest—"is about to knock you for a loop!"

Harry and Tucker had been sitting on the sidelines, staring in glazed fascination as the cat and the bird got more and more angry.

"Mousiekins," said Harry, just before he acted, "New York is really a wonderful city. Imagine being big enough to hold both Lulu and Miss Catherine. Ladies —*please!*"

"Ladies," said Tucker Mouse to himself, as he watched his friend try to separate them both. "Between two crazy ladies like Lulu Pigeon and Catherine Cat, a sane mouse could lose his mind!"

He was just about to suggest that the ladies be permitted to slug it out, when the coming brawl was abruptly interrupted—and not by Harry Cat.

# NINE

# Police!

Lulu was hauling off with one wing and Miss Catherine had the claws of both front paws extended. Violence was imminent, despite Harry's gentle efforts to prevent it. But before the first blow could be struck, a furor was heard from outside the pipe, in the subway station. There were shouts—from several human beings; there was running—impossible to tell how many people and animals running; and there was, unmistakably, at least one frantic barking dog!

"Harry!" Tucker yelled from the opening. "Come quick! It's Huppy—the cops are chasing him!"

The others crowded around the mouse, their own quarrels now completely forgotten.

Down the stairs from the street, half tumbling and half running, came Huppy. And behind him—three policemen, taking the stairs two at a time.

"Watch out for that dog!" shouted one officer to the people in the subway station. There weren't too many, this late at night, but the ones who were there were jumping like rabbits, out of the way.

"Mad dog!" a second policeman called.

*"Mad dog?"* Tucker echoed fearfully, with a terrified look at Harry. The cat's eyes answered him with an equal expression of horror.

Huppy bounded up in front of them and skidded to a halt. "Tucker—Harry—help!"

"You got rabies, kiddo?" said Lulu Pigeon curiously.

" 'Course not!" the puppy yelped. "In the park—we were fighting, earlier—not fighting really, just horsing around—I took on Big Louie—and all of a sudden the cops were there!" His breath came in pants. "They thought we were serious—and they don't much like stray dogs, anyway—and they *grabbed* me!"

"They're going to do it again!" shouted Tucker. "Run, Huppy!"

An officer made a dive for the dog, but seized empty air as he darted off in a flash of fur, zigzagging to escape, first right, then left, then left again. The officers were closing in. A final leap to the right—he was trapped. Not quite. He dashed between a policeman's legs, paused an instant, and disappeared. The policeman followed him into nothing.

"Oh, my gosh!" groaned Harry. "He's jumped down to the shuttle tracks."

"Let's hope she's not running on Track Number One tonight," said Lulu Pigeon.

# Police!

"Fly out there and give us bulletins!" commanded Tucker.

Lulu paddled through the air and settled on the railing above the shuttle tracks, where a dark tunnel led toward Grand Central Station.

"That, I take it, is Huppy. A fugitive from the law. If you think—"

Harry Cat forgot his manners. "For heaven's sake, shut up!" Then remembered them long enough to add, "Miss Catherine, please. Till we get this settled."

"Lulu!" called Tucker. "What's happening—"

They could hear her faintly: "Go, Huppy, go!"

In the black distance, shouting grew fainter and fainter. So did the barking. The shouting and barking stopped all at once. And changed—into fright. And changed direction—grew louder and louder.

"Uh-oh!" Lulu Pigeon left her perch. "She *is* on Number One!"

The animals in the drainpipe now had the chance to see something that very few New York human beings or animals have ever observed. And that is, a geyser of policemen erupting from the shuttle tracks and tumbling to safety. In back of them, in the biggest jump of his life—there's nothing like the lights and roar of a subway train to give you inspiration (when you're on the tracks, that is)—came Huppy. He landed right side up on the platform, unlike the officers, who were rolling around on their backs congratulating themselves and each other on still being alive. The dog ran to his friends.

"Are you *crazy*, Huppy?" said Tucker Mouse. "To jump—"

"I don't care! I'll do anything before I'll ever be caught again! That's what happened before. When the cops grabbed me, they put me in a police car. And then they shut the door! I waited there for hours while they chased the rest of the pack. But they didn't catch anybody else. And when they came back—" He suddenly stopped.

"Yes?" prompted Harry. "When they got back?"

"Well," Huppy stammered, "I was really awfully scared, you know—I could guess where they were taking me—so when the door to the car came open, and I saw the freedom outside, I—I—"

"Huppy," demanded Harry sternly, "what did you do?"

"Well—I sort of bit one cop, I guess." The dog's shaggy head hung down.

"That's grand!" said Tucker. "No wonder they think you have rabies."

"By the way, you guys," said Lulu Pigeon, perched now in the empty air above them, "I wouldn't want to upset anybody, but—*here they come again!*"

"Wait!" Harry grabbed a clawful of Huppy's tail and pulled him back out of his terrified flight. "It's no

good just running. We've got to get you hidden somewhere." His eyes rummaged the subway station. The
closets where the cleanup men stored their buckets and
mops were too far away, but—"There. That trash
basket! The rest of us'll create a diversion, and, Huppy,
you jump in. Lulu, bang around the policemen's
heads—"

"Groovy!" The pigeon clapped her wings.

"—but no pecking at eyes now. I'll pretend to make
friends and rub their legs. Tucker—just do whatever
comes to mind."

"My mad-mouse face!" decided Tucker. "It'll scare
them silly."

"And, Miss Catherine—"

"*I?*" exclaimed the Siamese in astonishment. "You
expect *me* to become involved with the police?"

"Yes, ma'am, I do! Just tiptoe out there on your little
pink paws and jump in the basket after Huppy and
cover him up with waste paper—"

"*Really,* Harry!"

"—and I'll apologize for my language later. Ready,
folks? Here we go!"

In a rush—and from nowhere, it seemed to the policemen—two cats, one pigeon, and one overactive mouse
surrounded the mad dog they were after. Despite her
misgivings, Miss Catherine had been swept along and
contributed her bit to the chaos.

"Hey, what are these animals doing?" said one officer.

"They got a zoo down here?" said another.

"Get away from me!" said the third. He shook his left leg, where Harry Cat was scratching his back and purring like a friendly dragon.

Lulu picked out the biggest, best-looking cop and perched on his shoulder. He twisted his head, uncertain of his feelings for pigeons, and looked at her with mixed emotions. She looked right back, but with romance in her beady black eyes, and murmured coyly, "Ooooo!" Her act proved sufficiently diverting to rivet him on the spot.

Tucker finally succeeded, after several squeaks, in attracting the attention of *his* officer and did his mad-mouse face. Which meant, he jumped up in the air as high as he could, stuck out his tongue, and crossed his eyes. It didn't exactly frighten the policeman—in fact, the only person it ever had frightened was Louisa, the timid, middle-aged lady who worked in the lunch stand—but it shocked him, nonetheless. (As well it might. Nothing like it had ever been seen by a member of the New York police force before.) He stared at Tucker in disbelief and said to his friends, "Will you look at this nutty mouse!"

That broke up Lulu. Her passion for the tall police-man evaporated in burbles of laughter. She got to *oo-oo-oo*ing so loudly and uncontrollably that, in order

to brace herself, she wrapped one wing around his neck and leaned her head against his head.

Under cover of all this outlandish activity, Huppy sneaked behind the officers, made a quiet leap into the trash basket and landed, with barely a rustle, in the midst of a pulled-apart copy of Sunday's *New York Times*. Which meant there was quite a lot of paper to hide in. Miss Catherine followed through the air— very gracefully, for a cat her age—and began to claw the loose sheets over him.

With much effort, the two policemen managed to detach themselves from their new-found friends Harry Cat and Lulu Pigeon. Harry was finally uncoiled like a snake from one officer's leg, and Lulu was unceremoniously scraped from a broad blue-uniformed shoulder. She was laughing too hard to fly, however, and fell down to the floor with a plop. Still shivering, she stood up and waddled into a hole in the wall. The cat pranced after her. And the mouse, after one last Halloween "Boo!", scooted in behind the two of them.

"Boy!" Tucker's victim—or rather, his audience— took off his cap and scratched his head. "You never know *what* you're gonna see when you've got the duty at night in Times Square."

"Where's the pooch?" said a fellow officer.

"Must have made his escape."

"Thank goodness," breathed Harry Cat, in the drainpipe.

# Police!

"Just save your thanks," whispered Tucker. "My cop is scrounging around the trash basket."

"Hey, you guys!" called Tucker's cop. "There's something in here." His hand flashed down and pulled up—"First mice, now this!"

"This" proved to be Miss Catherine Cat. The officer was holding her by the back of the neck. And although that is the way you are supposed to hold cats, Miss Catherine resented it terribly. Horatio would never have dared to manhandle her thus. She let her disapproval be known by wriggling and spitting fiercely.

"Stop laughing, Lulu!" said Harry.

"Boy, you two throw a great dinner party!" The pigeon propped herself against the wall.

"The party was an hour ago," said Tucker. "This is trouble!"

"Whatever it is, I love it!" gasped Lulu.

"So what'll we do with the fur ball?" asked Tucker's cop.

The other two thought a minute. Then Lulu's decided, "Better take it back to the station house."

"Yeah," Harry's agreed. "We lose a dog—we catch a cat."

To Miss Catherine, the "station house" sounded very much like "jail." Her legs flew out, stiff; her fur crackled with electricity; her spitting changed into wild shrieks: Miss Catherine became a bolt of feline lightning, held at arm's length by a wary policeman.

"Wow! Some wildcat!"

"Harry," urged Tucker quietly, "you've got to do something!"

"Aw, let 'em take her," Lulu advised. "A night in the pokey'll do her good!"

"*Harry*—they're leaving."

"Well, I hate to interfere with due process of law," said Harry Cat, "but—"

He dashed from the drainpipe, slowed, slipped up behind the policemen, who were now on the stairs leading out of the station—and soundlessly mixed himself up with the feet of the one who was carrying Miss Catherine.

"Hey!"

"Watch it! There's another one."

Down came the officer, still holding Miss Catherine aloft. She yanked herself free, spun twice in the air, but with all her cat's instincts still functioning, she landed right side up, on feet that already were running. In a flash she was down the stairs—in the drainpipe—safe.

Harry wrestled his way through grasping hands. He gained open space. With a rush he, too, was among his friends.

For a while, without much enthusiasm, the policemen searched at the pipe's opening. Tucker's cop was even brave enough to reach in his hand—but not too

# Police!

far: where there was a mouse there might be rats. The animals backed against the wall.

"You want me to peck that hand?" offered Lulu.

"No!" whispered Harry. "Just hush up, that's all."

Before long—"The heck with it!" said Lulu's cop. Harry's gave the opening a futile kick. "There's something strange going on in there."

He was right, of course. But not even the police know all the strange things that go on in New York.

# TEN

# Max

An hour later the animals were all huddled in a parking lot near the corner of Forty-second Street and Tenth Avenue. While Tucker stood guard—on the lookout for policemen and other overly inquisitive people—Harry had coaxed Huppy out of the trash basket. It took a great deal of cajoling and reassuring before the dog's fur-covered eyes appeared beneath the book-review section of the Sunday *New York Times*. After much encouragement he jumped out, and everyone padded, on paws and claws, as fast and silently as they could, away from Times Square.

Silently, that is, except Lulu. She insisted on flying ahead of them and squawking warnings—"Squad car ahead!" "Two bums in a doorway on the right!"—at the top of her voice. Despite her help, they escaped from the crowded blocks to an area where even Forty-second Street was deserted.

"Well—this is it," said Harry, with a flick of finality in his tail. "We've got to decide what to do."

"Before your deliberations begin," said Miss Catherine, "I shall bid you good night." For most of the hour since her unladylike escape—the indignity of it still rankled—she had crouched in a cranny of the drainpipe, trembling, but now that Tenth Avenue stretched ahead of her, the path to the safety and comfort of Horatio's apartment, her old arrogance returned. "*So* pleased to have met you all!" Her smile glittered as cheerfully as the ice in the parking lot behind them. "Such a nice meal, Mr. Mouse! Harry—I trust that I'll see you again. But give me a couple of days to recuperate. I haven't had so much excitement since the apartment two floors down caught fire!" She laughed—at nothing especially funny, perhaps just at her own embarrassment, to be leaving them in the lurch.

"Now hold on, Miss Catherine!" said Tucker. "Do you mean to say that you're going to walk off and just leave the little dog sitting here?"

"What is this little dog to me?" She glared toward Huppy, but her eyes jumped away from his woolly face, as if there was something to hurt her there. "What is he, I mean, except a source of great injury—I'll be lame for a week!—and almost arrested, and—" And she went on, not looking at anyone in particular, but insisting that it would not *do!* Huppy couldn't live with her and Horatio, not even in the basement. No! It simply would not do.

This was the first time Huppy had heard about the

plan to move him to the Upper West Side. He listened until Miss Catherine had run out of excuses—the breakable china in the apartment, the janitor finding him in the cellar—and finished shaking her head. Then he said, downcast but determined, "She's right. I won't do."

"I said 'it'—" the Siamese corrected him.

"But I want to thank you anyway, Miss Catherine."

"Thank me—" She glared at him, almost angrily. "For what?"

"For pulling the papers over me. The cops would've caught me for sure."

"That was *nothing!*" The Siamese stamped an elegant paw. "Such a nuisance this all is—really!"

"And I'm sorry you got hurt."

"Oh, it isn't that bad. I daresay I won't be lame for a week."

Even Lulu knew enough not to break a long silence during which Miss Catherine fretted and fidgeted, and did not go home.

At last she said, "Young fellow—what'll you do now? Go back to the pack?"

"No, ma'am. We're down here on Tenth Avenue —I'm going to my alley. Maybe I'll think of something there. If Harry helps me, anyway, I can. But I'm finished with the pack."

"Says who?"

The animals all jumped at the sound: a voice of silken authority that came from in back of a run-down

Buick. Out of the night, his smile first, like the Cheshire cat, Max materialized. "Sure you're coming back with us. I don't waste my time for nothing, Hup."

Harry Cat was the first to shake off his surprise. "Where did *you* come from?" he asked suspiciously.

"I saw him bust free in Bryant Park and followed those Looney Tune cops."

"You didn't help much!" said Tucker.

"What could I do?" Max shrugged. "And why risk my fur? I hung around Times Square. If the blue boys collared him again—good night, little dog. If they didn't, in future he'll know enough not to get busted. That's how a kid learns to stay alive in this city. I tailed you all down here." He narrowed his eyes on Huppy. "What did you bring these clowns with you for?"

"We are *not* clowns, sir!" burst in Miss Catherine. She was very relieved, without knowing it, to have found somebody besides herself to be irritated at. "You're the brute that Harry's told me about! Well, just you let me tell you, brute, if it wasn't for us—" She fell silent beneath the dog's stony stare of disbelief. No one had called him a brute before. "Boss," yes. "Sir," yes—by some of his more frightened subordinates. But never, ever, "brute."

"Who is the battle-ax?" Max asked softly.

"Don't you *dare* refer to me in those terms! Why— why—"

"Look, Kate," said Lulu, who knew Max better than any of them, "just cool it—okay?"

"If the ruffian thinks he can call me names!" Miss Catherine was sputtering with rage. "Why, he ought to be in the dog pound himself—with all the bad habits he's been teaching this puppy!" If Miss Catherine had been a lady now, instead of only a lady cat, she would have been shaking a furious finger right under Max's nose. "I've a good mind to howl right now—yes, I have!—although I haven't howled for years—and summon those three officers."

At that, hardly looking at her, as a human being might flick off a fly, Max lifted a paw and cuffed Miss Catherine.

It didn't hurt, despite the gasp of fear and shock with which the other animals started forward. But for Miss Catherine the blow was worse than pain. She'd been insulted—deeply, truly insulted. Even the fright of being gripped in the none-too-gentle hand of the law was nothing compared to this. With almost a kitten's helplessness, she turned away and began to cry.

For the others, her tears were dreadful to see. It *is* awful when a real lady cries—either human ladies or dogs or cats. It makes you feel ashamed and angry and powerless all at once, the way a person always feels when, against all written and unwritten rules, something happens that simply should not.

A gap of embarrassment held everyone—even Max —for a moment. Bad-mannered, cruel, casual, he too realized what he'd done. He forced a chuckle that stuck in his throat.

Then a second incredible thing took place. Without

warning, without knowing where his own teeth were going, Huppy leaped at Max and nipped his nose.

The big dog didn't make a move—didn't bark, didn't growl, didn't bare his own fangs. He just stared at the puppy. Then breathed in slowly, and softly stated what were only the facts: "I could tear you apart."

"I know you could." Huppy backed away.

"I could wipe up this street with you."

"I know you could, Max."

It was like those times when a little kid has dared to hit a big kid. He knows that the big kid can beat him up—and probably will—and all he can do, with a fearful and partly apologetic expression, is to wait for his fate.

Harry sprang his claws, Tucker bared what little teeth he had, and Lulu Pigeon was wondering if she ought to act first—fly up and begin to peck Max's head. She would have been slaughtered if she had. And so would the mouse and the cat, if they'd even so much as made a move. The dog was big and crafty enough, and had won enough fights, to take the three of them on at once, and Huppy and Miss Catherine too, if she could stop crying. He could have scattered bloody feathers and fur for blocks along Tenth Avenue.

He unhooked his eyes from Huppy's, turned his back on them all, and loped up Forty-second Street. And did not look back.

In the silence that steadied everybody's relief, no

one could explain why Max had left. Out of privacy and a strange respect for him, nobody even tried.

At last Harry said, "I'll walk you home, Miss Catherine."

"No, no!" She had stopped her crying and was back to fretting like her old self again. "It simply won't *do*, that's all. He can't go back to an alley, can he? Such a nuisance! Really!"

"He can't fit in the drainpipe," Tucker Mouse reminded no one in particular.

"You'll just have to come up to the apartment house, and stay in the basement. For only tonight, mind you!"

There were mumbles of appreciation.

Lulu took her post in the air. "Three guys to the right who look suspicious!"

"Thank you very much," said Tucker. "But you can go home now, Lulu. We won't be—"

"No, man!" yelled the pigeon. "I won't abandon you now!"

"Lulu, do us a favor!" Tucker called up. "Abandon us!"

But she didn't. She guided them, at the top of her lungs, all the way uptown.

One plump pigeon up ahead, two fairish-sized cats, an extra-large puppy, and a rather small mouse—all in all, they made quite an odd procession, trudging through the winter night.

# ELEVEN

# A Cellarful of Memories

The basement of Mr. Smedley's apartment house was a clutter of cast-off things that the tenants above didn't really need but couldn't bear to throw away. (There were a few mice already living there, but when they heard the new arrivals clambering in through the broken window, they scurried into the walls through their holes and stayed hidden until the cellar was theirs again.) Tucker felt very much at home in the jumble and proceeded to do some heartfelt scrounging as the animals waited for morning.

No one could sleep—except Lulu, of course. She was able to take the wildest night's activities in her flight and said that if nobody minded she'd like to sack out for a couple of hours. But as soon as she got her head under her wing she started to snore so loudly that it was feared she'd wake the janitor, who had his apartment at the front end of the basement. Harry and Tucker shook her awake, made her waddle into a cardboard box on its side, and flipped the cover over on her. Inside, she sawed wood to her heart's content.

Huppy did a little exploring too. But unlike Tucker, who used his claws to turn things over, Huppy, since he was a dog, limited his investigations to some interested sniffing. "Here's something that smells like Miss Catherine!" he said.

"Smells?" Miss Catherine arched an eyebrow.

"Mind your manners," Harry reminded the dog.

"I mean, it smells nice," said Huppy. "Kind of perfumy."

"Well, for land's sake!" Miss Catherine went over to the corner where Huppy was nosing around. "It's my good old mat!"

Her good old mat was an oval hooked rug. "That was yours?" said Harry. "It's big enough for a—that is, it's pretty big for a cat, isn't it?"

"Oh, my, yes. The edges fell way over the sides of the sewing basket. But Mrs. Smedley finished hooking it the very same day that I was acquired—at the Siamese Specialty Shop on Fifty-seventh Street—and she decided that instead of using it for a rug it would be my mat." Miss Catherine laughed. "So impetuous Horatio's mother was—quite unlike her son in many ways. I remember that day very well. She dumped over the contents of the sewing basket, put the rug inside, as much as would fit, and then snugged me in, too! 'There!' she said. 'That can be Miss Catherine's mat.'

It was she who named me, you know—right then. And quick as a wink I felt at home."

"Home," purred Harry.

"I've always wondered what happened to it. One day it was gone." She reached out a paw and touched the mat gently, as if there was something alive in it. "Horatio must have thought that a rug wouldn't do for me. But I think it would—don't you, Harry?"

"If you wanted it to," he rumbled softly.

Miss Catherine's eyes picked over the boxes and loosely tied bundles that littered the basement, seeking and sorting familiar things, selecting memories.

"Miss Catherine—there's still a couple of hours left, if you want to go upstairs and sleep."

"No, no." She shook the suggestion out of her whiskers. "*I* won't abandon you either. Perhaps I'll just browse awhile down here."

Harry Cat went off to one side and curled up. His eyes closed until only a crack was left, but he was a very long way from sleep. Through the slit of vision he watched Miss Catherine carefully as she wandered through her past—a favorite bowl, cracked, for her cat food, a chipped saucer that had been for her milk—going deeper and deeper into her kittenhood.

"Look, Harry! My bell." She tinkled a little silver bell with a ribbon attached to it. "At one time Horatio got it into his head that I must have a bell. Well, I put my paw down at *that*, I can tell you."

In an upper corner of the cellar a dirty window showed a patch of night. A silver crescent, dropping westward, slid into view. And a single low note sounded through the cellar.

"Good Lord!" said Miss Catherine. "What's that?"

"Huppy, shh!" warned Harry.

"Come here," Miss Catherine summoned the dog, who padded up in front of her. "Was that you howling?"

"Yes, ma'am."

"I thought dogs only howled at full moons."

"I like to howl at all different moons. I'm sorry if it bothered you."

"Oh, no—it's quite pretty."

"Us dogs think so."

" 'We dogs,' " Miss Catherine corrected him. "Let's hear it again."

Huppy tried another note, a higher one this time, and his voice cracked. He gulped in embarrassment. Harry and Miss Catherine shot a look at each other and shared a chuckle.

"Guess who's growing up," said Harry.

"Bend toward me, Huppy," the Siamese said. She sat up on her hind legs. "Such a thicket your hair is! Can you really see through it?"

"Oh, yes." Huppy bowed his head to the elderly cat. "I switch around till I get an opening."

"I think it might help if—" She sprung her claws.

"Hold still now." And started to comb Huppy's hair.

"Ow!"

"Hold *still*, I say! There's a monstrous knot here. There—isn't that better?"

"Yes, ma'am." Huppy looked at her somewhat sheepishly—which was perfectly natural, since he was part sheep dog—through his now combed if still somewhat sooty hair.

Miss Catherine had her right paw lifted, to give him one finishing brush—but suddenly she pulled away and stamped that paw on the floor. "Oh, really! *really!* This *is* too much!" She turned on Harry, eyes flashing with what he knew was not rage. "All right, Harry Cat—you win!"

135

"I, Miss Catherine?" said Harry, with his own eyes as wide and innocent as a cat's eyes can ever be. (Not very innocent, at that.) "Win what?"

"You know perfectly well!" she fussed at him. "I shall try to inveigle Horatio into letting the animal—"

"Me?"

"Hush, child! Yes, you. Inveigle Horatio into letting the animal live with us! It won't be easy. If you think that I've been difficult—"

"What's the matter?" Tucker Mouse, who had heard her outburst, came pattering up. Without so much as looking at him, Harry silently flattened him to the floor and went on paying strict attention to everything Miss Catherine was saying.

"—well, you don't know Horatio! He has to be won over, too." She glanced up at the window: gray light filtered through its screen of dirt. "We'll be out in the park at ten this morning."

"That may be too early."

"It *isn't* too early! We have no lessons on Tuesday morning—"

"Harry—if you wouldn't mind—let me up!"

"—and I only have to tap the door to let him know when I want my walk. In the meantime"—Miss Catherine prepared to go—"I advise *you*, Harry Cat, and *you*, Tucker Mouse—"

"Thanks, Harry. Uff—what a paw!"

"—to think of some way that this woolly young fellow can be made absolutely indispensable to Horatio Smedley's happiness! Good morning! And I'll see you later!"

"What's up?" yawned Lulu Pigeon sleepily, as she ambled into the conversation.

"Huppy gets to live with Miss Catherine after all," explained Tucker. "At least, that's what we hope."

"Hey, groovy!" Lulu clapped a wing around Miss Catherine's shoulder and patted her on the back. "But what took you so long, Kate?"

Miss Catherine glared—then sighed, and looked toward heaven, and left.

## TWELVE

# Riverside Park

Riverside Park is a narrow band of trees, shrubs, dirt, and other valuable things wedged by concrete against the Hudson River on the Upper West Side of Manhattan. The great power of the place—it is like a huge magnet that draws everything toward it—is, of course, the steady and majestic Hudson. Even the trees seem to bend toward its beauty. Polluted though the river is, its current—deep, wide, strong—leads people to think of things that change and yet always remain the same. It is curiously comforting, but it makes a person feel very small. And it makes small animals feel even smaller.

They were all lined up on the promenade, a sort of broad sidewalk that runs beside the river's edge, peering through the openings of an iron railing. For a long time no one had said a word—not even Lulu. That's another of the river's strengths: it makes all pauses and silences feel peaceful, not embarrassing.

Splashes of wind tufted Huppy's fur. He craned through the bars and stared at the water. "It looks alive."

"It looks cold," said Tucker. "See?—ice." Broken white chunks were scraping against the promenade's cement foundation.

Although it already was March and the day was sunny, the sky brilliant, and the river's surface dancing with light, harsh winter had not given up. The chill air pierced through the animals' fur and made their eyes water. There were weeks before the tight earth behind them would toss, like someone shaking off dreams, and then, at the touch of one warm day, wake up.

Harry judged by the sun it was almost midmorning. "You remember what we told you now, Huppy."

"You didn't tell me much," complained Huppy.

"We said—just be charming!" Tucker airily waved a claw.

"Yes, but how do you be charming?" Huppy waved his own paw and hit Tucker in the head by mistake.

"Not like that!"

"Do a real doggy thing!" suggested Lulu. "Like on television. Go up and lap old Smedley's hand, and stare at him stupidly and say 'Woof!' "

"Grand!" said Harry Cat skeptically.

"Say!—here's a great gimmick!" Lulu's inspiration was now out of control. "Get a stick and drop it in front of Smedley. All dogs like to chase sticks, don't they?"

"Better they should chase pigeons," grumbled Tucker Mouse.

"You drop the stick, you prance around in front of him, do cute little things with your paws—he throws the stick, you bring it back, and there you are! Buddies!"

"Unless he hits me on the head with the stick," said Huppy dubiously.

Harry Cat was twitching his whiskers. "You know, that stick idea is not bad. If all else fails, Huppy, try it."

"*What* else?" the dog asked frantically. "You haven't told me."

Lulu was sitting on top of the railing and could see deeper into the park than the others. "Here they come! And will you look at that outfit Miss Catherine has on!"

Down a walk that curved to the promenade came Miss Catherine Cat and Mr. Horatio Smedley. The cat was leading him—perhaps he thought it was the other way around—at the end of a bright red leather leash, and she was wearing—in fact, they both were wearing —plaid sweaters.

"Identical sweaters!" said Tucker. "*Yich!* A dog may be too late for him, Huppy."

"I didn't know cats could have sweaters," said Huppy.

"In this city," Tucker explained, "everybody gets clothes. Except mice."

"If we get Huppy settled, Mousiekins, I'll knit you a sweater myself!" said Harry. "They're sitting down. Okay, Huppy, do your stuff."

"I'm scared."

"Get out there and charm, you lovable mutt!" Lulu Pigeon encouraged him. And then added, with great expectations of the coming scene, *"Oo! oo! oo!"*

Harry and Tucker and the chortling pigeon retired behind a screen of shrubs while Huppy shuffled awkwardly up to the bench where Miss Catherine and Mr. Smedley were sitting. (Naturally, she was sitting on the bench beside him, the ground being chilly, dirty, and beneath her dignity.)

The dog sat down on his haunches and stared at Mr. Smedley, who eyed him back suspiciously. Miss Catherine, too, was watching him. She began to tap a paw with impatience. At last Huppy worked up enough courage to cough and clear his throat—Mr. Smedley lifted both feet—and get out a feeble "Woof."

"Pure charm!" whispered Lulu.

"Shut up, Lulu," said Tucker automatically, without taking his eyes from the bench.

Mr. Smedley made flicking motions with one wrist and said peevishly, "Shoo! Shoo!"—as if Huppy was nothing but a lump of soot that he could brush away.

Huppy sighed, and tried again, louder: *"Woof!"*

"The kid's got a limited vocabulary," commented Lulu Pigeon.

"*You're* the one who suggested 'Woof'!" muttered Harry, beneath his breath.

"Look," said Tucker. "He thinks Huppy is after Miss Catherine."

Mr. Smedley, alarmed by that rather vociferous woof, had taken his precious cat in his lap and was shaking a finger at Huppy. "Go 'way now, you! Go right away! We don't want you here—do we, Puss-puss?"

Miss Catherine peered over a knee. "Young fellow," she miaowed, "you'll have to do better than that!" (Of course, to Mr. Smedley it only sounded like a cat's miaowing—in complete agreement with his own opinion. Like most human beings, he heard only what he wanted to hear in the conversation of animals.)

"Well, I'm doing my best," whimpered Huppy.

"All right, we accept your apology for all that barking," Mr. Smedley sniffed. "But run along. Fft! Fft!"

"You *had* better leave us alone a minute," miaowed Miss Catherine. "I'll try to change Horatio's mood."

"Okay, Miss Catherine." Forlornly, Huppy wandered off, as she snuggled down deeper in Horatio's lap and began to purr.

"Will you look at her butter that sucker up!" exclaimed Tucker Mouse with admiration.

"Oh, my!" Mr. Smedley purred back at his cat. "Puss-puss is in a good mood today!" Miss Catherine arched her head under his hand for more stroking. "Would she like to hear some poetry?"

"Mmm!" purred Miss Catherine.

"Poetry! Whoopee!" chortled Lulu. "I know: shut up."

Mr. Smedley pulled a paperback anthology of *Famous Poems* out of one of his pockets and began to read his favorite: "Ode to the West Wind," by Shelley. He loved the poem and read it very dramatically, with many expressive gestures of the hand that wasn't holding the book.

While the reading proceeded—"Where's Huppy?" said Harry suddenly.

"Disappeared off in those bushes beyond the bench," said Lulu. "I think he's looking for a—here he comes! Ooo, now," she cooed when she saw what he was carrying.

"That's no stick!" blurted Tucker Mouse. "That's a *log!*"

The dog was holding in his mouth neither stick nor log, but a fairly big branch that had crashed off an elm tree during an ice storm in January. It was so large his jaws could barely get a grip and so heavy he was weaving from side to side, like a drunken man, to balance it. But it was all he'd been able to find. With dogged determination he lurched toward the bench.

" 'O Wind,' " voice rising rapturously, and unaware of Huppy's approach, Mr. Smedley recited the last lines of the "Ode to the West Wind." " 'If Winter comes, can Spring be far be—' *Ow!*" Huppy dropped the branch on his foot.

"Tim-ber!" shouted Lulu Pigeon.

"Mousiekins"—Harry Cat let a deep sigh escape—"I think you and I had better start looking for a very much larger drainpipe."

Mr. Smedley was hopping around on one foot, Miss Catherine had jumped to the ground, and Huppy, exhausted by all his effort, was sitting, panting.

"And what's the meaning of this?" said the Siamese.

"He throws the stick, I get it, and we become friends," explained Huppy. "It was Lulu's idea."

"I might have guessed!" She switched her tail. "I think, from now on, you had best leave matters to me. And first off, show Horatio how much you like me." Instinctively, and without one second's delay, Huppy gave her a big lap-kiss. "Really!" she huffed. "That's *not* what I had in mind!"

"I'm sorry, Miss—"

"Well, let it pass. Now demonstrate to Horatio how compatible you are."

"I don't know what that means," mumbled Huppy, who was feeling quite futile this afternoon.

"Oh, for mercy's sake—shake hands! All dogs can do that, can't they?"

Obediently Huppy held out one paw. Mr. Smedley was sitting on the bench again; he had taken off a shoe and was rubbing his foot. "I will *not* shake hands!"

"Miaow," said Miss Catherine.

"Oh. Does Puss-puss want to see Daddy shake hands with this raggedy dog?"

"Miaow!"

Very gingerly Mr. Smedley took Huppy's paw between his thumb and index finger and wiggled it. Then he flicked away three specks of dust, duty done.

"Now show him you want to play throw-and-fetch," whispered Miss Catherine.

Huppy nosed the branch, ran away a few feet, barked, ran back, and looked up expectantly. "I will *not* throw that thing," said Horatio firmly.

"Mi-*aow*," said Miss Catherine, even more firmly.

"We ought to make a movie of this," said Tucker Mouse.

"Shut up," said Lulu Pigeon. "We could call it 'How to Train Your Pet.'"

Much to Mr. Smedley's surprise, a game of throw-and-fetch began which was quite a lot of fun. The last time he'd had any exercise was two and a half years ago, when he'd read an article in *The New York Times* about the benefits of jogging. He had hoisted himself up from his reading chair and run once around the reservoir in Central Park, and that had sufficed for the next twenty-eight months. But now, in the crisp air, he found it was quite delightful—exhilarating, in fact —to throw that branch and watch the dog run after it and come tottering back with it in his mouth. He let Miss Catherine off her leash, for private prowls or to sit on the sidelines and watch the sport, and walked up on a little hill, to a better throwing place.

As for Huppy—this was the first time he'd ever played with a human being, and he enjoyed the running, the lugging, the barking, the pouncing on the branch, even more than Mr. Smedley did. Indeed, he became so excited about the game he forgot himself completely. On his fifth retrieve, instead of simply dropping the branch, he jumped up—"just to give it to him!" he later explained—and propped his paws on Mr. Smedley's waist.

Back fell the man, on a patch of ice beneath him; forward fell Huppy, on top of him; and down they both rolled, kicking to disentangle each other, to the foot of the slope, which, though small, provided enough dirt to cover them both.

"Oh! oh! oh!" Mr. Smedley exploded in puffs of anger. He threw the branch—*at* Huppy this time, not for him to fetch. Immediately he was sorry, being by nature a gentle man, but he really detested dirt and could feel that even his face was covered.

The branch hit Huppy in the rump. He yelped and, knowing all was lost, ran off.

Ran back to his friends, where Miss Catherine, too, was sitting. "I only—I only—"

"We know what you only," said Harry Cat. He gave

Huppy a fatherly pat on the back. (Cats—and some human beings, too—love children most when their situation seems hopeless.)

Stony silence.

Harry chipped at it. "Well—"

Four voices asked, all at once, "Well what?"

"Just one thing left." Harry looked toward the river. "Heroism. What man could resist a heroic dog who life-saved somebody?"

"Great idea!" squawked Lulu. "But how do we get Smedley into the river?"

"It isn't going to be Mr. Smedley."

" 'Course not!" Tucker Mouse took up the plan. "Better yet—a little old lady! She's walking along the promenade, I scare her, she falls in—"

"And no little old ladies," said Harry. "No human beings at all. Too dangerous. He's still only a pretty small dog. By the way, Huppy, this means you jump into the Hudson River. That okay with you?"

"It's got to be okay," said Huppy dogfully. "Whatever happens, I'd rather end up in the river than back in the alley."

"If not a human being—who?" asked Lulu Pigeon.

"Me!" said Harry. "I jump in, Huppy pulls me out—it's our only chance."

More silence—even thicker now.

"I'm afraid that won't quite do." Miss Catherine had been sitting apart, watching, thinking—thinking hard.

"I fear that Horatio isn't the sort of man to concern himself with—beg pardon, Harry—the fate of a stray alley cat."

"Then there's no hope," said Harry.

"No," she contradicted him softly. "The strategy is excellent." Her tail lifted gracefully into the air. "And it just so happens there *is* one person in the world that he loves enough for the whole thing to work." That tail coiled down and ended in a perfect curve around her own legs.

"Miss Catherine! Are you crazy?" exploded Harry Cat. "I, too, beg pardon, but a lady of your age—"

"It's really quite perfect, you know." She wasn't even listening, as she tested the wind with her whiskers. "He's always warned me, all these years, to stay away from the promenade when I'm not on the leash. For fear a blast would carry me over. It's good and gusty today. Young fellow, can you swim?"

"I don't know, Miss Catherine," Huppy explained. "I've never tried."

"Neither have I, child. But we'll soon find out."

"Miss Catherine, I will *not* permit—"

"Oh, won't you, indeed?" Before Harry's restraining paw could touch her back, Miss Catherine had vanished beneath it and was halfway down to the promenade. Huppy galloped after her. So did the others.

She reached the railing, waited a second for a suitable gust, let out her most ear-tearing Siamese scream—

disappeared. Huppy didn't stop running. Feet still scrambling in empty air, he sailed through the opening Miss Catherine had chosen and dropped from sight. Harry reached the edge first, just in time to see the gray Hudson close over his bushy tail.

"Where *are* they?" squealed Tucker.

"There!" Lulu wing-pointed out Miss Catherine's head, which choking, coughing, broke the surface. A moment later Huppy's did, too—several yards behind her. The current, strong fingerless fist of water, had seized them both and was rushing them southward, separated. Those watching on the bank could see from their helpless bobbing—over and over, into and under chunks of ice—that the two of them were almost unconscious, thrust out of their senses by the sudden shock of icy water. It has happened very often to men, to dogs—even to calculating cats—that *deciding* to be a hero and *finding* yourself in a burning room or a frigid flood are two quite different experiences.

Huppy got back some self-control first and dog-paddled like mad toward Miss Catherine. A blade of ice flashed past his nose, and a thread of crimson went tangling in the water ahead of him.

"Look!" shouted Tucker.

"I can see!" said Harry. "He's bleeding."

"No, *look!*"

Harry followed his friend's voice, which went up. And there, balancing on the railing above them, stood

Horatio Smedley. He had heard Miss Catherine's shriek, all right. For a second he poised, then grabbed his nose—jumped, without a sound.

"That's something I didn't expect!" said Tucker.

"Impetuous"—Harry remembered. "He takes after his mother, after all."

Three bodies were now toiling in the river beneath the animals.

And around them, magnetized first by the scream and then by the man on the railing, people had begun to collect. Children, nursemaids, men and women strolling—they were gathered into a shouting knot that drifted down the promenade, parallel to those who were drifting in the turbulent Hudson.

Voices: "Why doesn't somebody call the police?"

"I hear—"

"Somebody has!"

From Riverside Drive, which is beside the park, came the fearful howl of a squad car. In the animals' ears it was sheer melody.

Huppy reached Miss Catherine, and took the back of her neck in his mouth as gently as he could. They were brushed against the foundations of the promenade. Which was fortunate in a way, because, clawing, scratching at the concrete, he was able to hold them there long enough for Mr. Smedley to reach them. The three were now one blob of life that was fighting against the deadly river.

They lost their fight temporarily, and were swept farther on. The promenade ended. At its corner the crowd hung above them, watching—Tucker and Harry and Lulu, too, but no one noticed them, pressed down in front of the packed, excited throng.

Beyond a stretch of open water, where cat and dog and man were spun, rose the pilings of an abandoned warehouse. Mr. Smedley, holding Huppy's neck, who was holding Miss Catherine's, swam, with the arm that was free, toward it. The current, a lifeless friend now, as it had been a lifeless enemy, pressed them all against a thick wooden support, and held them there.

"They're safe!" said Tucker.

"Not till the cops get them out," said Harry.

"There one goes!" Lulu clapped her wings as an officer with a rope around him jumped into the river and swam downstream.

"Harry, as long as everybody is jumping in the Hudson River—"

"You stay right where you are!" Harry planted his paw on Tucker's tail. "For a cat the cops might go in. For a dog, perhaps. For a man, absolutely! For a mouse, they'd be glad to get rid of you."

"You wouldn't be insulting, please, Harry."

All watched, with cheers, comments, and hollered suggestions, as the rescue was brought to completion. (Many wished it had taken more time. There's nothing like somebody else's danger to perk up a dull weekday.)

In a few minutes a policeman, a music teacher, and a cat and dog were watering the promenade. "Better get home and dry off quick," said the cop.

"I will, officer." Mr. Smedley stopped kissing Miss Catherine. "And thank you very much."

"Think nothing of it. Beats chasing burglars any day." The cop chucked Miss Catherine under the chin. And stooped to pet Huppy on the head. "And dry off your pets, too. Animals catch cold as easy as people. This dog's got a cut—" Blood still was leaking from Huppy's nose. He had to keep spitting out red drops.

"That isn't my dog," said Mr. Smedley.

"Whose is he, then?"

"I don't know."

The dog sat motionless by Mr. Smedley's heel. For the first time the music teacher noticed, through a crack in the matted fur, that his eyes were pale blue— a questioning, rather distant blue—not pleading, merely wondering: the color of the late-winter sky above them.

"He's got no collar. I'll have to take him in."

"Take him where?"

"The dog pound. Because he's got no collar. Nobody owns him."

Mr. Smedley frowned. He looked at Miss Catherine. She also frowned, and announced, "Miaow!"

"Come on, pooch," the policeman called Huppy.

"No, *no!*" Horatio Smedley fretted. "That simply will not *do!*"

# THIRTEEN

# Happy

It was afternoon of a dozy day in April—the first really irresistible day, when work and worry dissolve and the warm air whispers disturbingly, "Spring has finally arrived, it is right outside the window!" Rich sunlight filtered through lazily drifting curtains, and Jimmy Lebovski could not get through "The Spinning Wheel."

"Jimmy," his piano teacher sighed, "your left hand doesn't seem to be on speaking terms with your right."

"I know," said Jimmy wearily. "It keeps forgetting where the fingers go."

"Perhaps it's thinking of picking flowers."

"It's thinking of my catcher's mitt," said Jimmy.

"Once more, please!" The teacher tapped the top of the grand piano with a little stick with which he kept time. "And then you can take *both* hands off to the playing field. One, two, three, *and*—!"

"Mr. Smedley"—Jimmy broke off the opening bars of "The Spinning Wheel," which had not gotten off to all that good a start anyway—"you know what might help?"

"I can't imagine!" Mr. Smedley's curiosity was larger than life-size.

"Well, if I could see the dog—"

"Oh. The dog. You think *he* might inspire you, do you?"

"He could."

Mr. Smedley squelched a smile, moistened his lips, and whistled a melody. It happened to be the very sweet tune that begins the sextet from the opera *Lucia di Lammermoor,* but Jimmy Lebovski didn't know that, and neither did the huge dog that bounded into the music room from the open door to the hall.

"Gosh! He's grown."

"Indeed he has." Mr. Smedley shook his head. "I sometimes wonder if he'll ever *stop* growing." This dog, who might never stop growing, appeared to have cornered all the hair on the Upper West Side. It floated around him in a gray and white cloud. But at least it was clean; the white patches of fur sparkled like freshly washed linen in the afternoon sun. He also seemed to have something of a monopoly on local high spirits. After a customary lap at Mr. Smedley's cheek, which the music teacher held out obligingly, he put his forepaws up on the piano bench and did the same for Jimmy, who enjoyed large dogs much more than piano lessons.

"Can he sit on the bench, Mr. Smedley?"

"I suppose *that* would make you a concert pianist."

"Please, Mr. Smedley!"

Jimmy needn't have pleaded, because the big dog did not wait for his master's permission. He jumped up on the bench beside the pupil, sat down, and stared at the piano keys. And woofed.

"He wants to sing, Mr. Smedley!"

"Young man! 'The Spinning Wheel,' if you please."

"After he sings, Mr. Smedley! Honest, I promise!"

"Oh, very well." With an eagerness that he tried to make sound like impatience, Mr. Smedley plunked middle C on the piano. And the dog let out a long and delightful howl. By no means was it middle or any other C, but it was enough to send Jimmy into hoots of laughter.

"Again!" he begged.

"No! Play!" commanded the music teacher.

The dog howled again. So did Jimmy.

"Not *you!*" Mr. Smedley shooed the big fluffy cushion of a dog away. "Run along now, Happy. *Whssht!* That's right—"

"Happy?" said Tucker Mouse. "He calls him Happy?"

In the hall, just out of Mr. Smedley's sight, Harry Cat, Lulu, Miss Catherine, and Tucker were gathered to watch and listen to the concert in the music room.

# Happy

"Isn't it a coincidence?" Miss Catherine asked. "But a few days after we'd gotten him back here—and washed him and brushed him and made him feel at home—the dog seemed to enjoy himself so much that Horatio decided to call him Happy. Of course he asked me about it first, but I let it pass, being near enough to the name you gave him."

Happy-Huppy bounded into the hall. "How was I, Miss Catherine?"

"Quite good, child." She patted the dog on his lowered head. "I still think there's a little room for improvement."

"He could be called some worse things than Happy," said Lulu. "If he'd stayed with the pack, we'd be calling him Hippy. *Oo! oo! oo!*"

Tucker groaned and made a face, but since this was a special occasion, nobody begrudged the kookoo bird a pun that she at least considered hilarious. (She'd been saving it up for weeks.)

This afternoon was the first time since the great events in Riverside Park that Tucker and Harry had been invited to the Smedley apartment. Lulu, who was turning into a regular carrier pigeon, tried to keep them informed about Huppy's progress, but Tucker, tending to nerves as he did, could not be satisfied by her rambling accounts. They consisted mostly of jokes, laughs, and descriptions of everything Miss Catherine saved up for her. The cat and the pigeon had become quite chummy lately. Miss Catherine had even miaowed Mr. Smedley into setting up a bird feeder outside the kitchen window. Lulu had had to beat up two starlings—an episode which she described at great length—but the feeder and its contents were now her own.

After three weeks had passed, Tucker Mouse announced that, ready or not, he was coming up to see Huppy. So Miss Catherine decided that she might as well have everybody "to tea." But fortunately, "tea" was not tea. It was, all laid out in saucers on the kitchen floor while Horatio gave his piano lessons, cat food for Harry—Miss Catherine had made a selection of her own favorite flavors; the usual crumbs from Mr. Smedley's breakfast English muffin for Lulu; and the remains of a cube steak that he'd had for lunch for Tucker.

But strange to say, the mouse had other things than food on his mind. "Are you happy, Huppy?" he asked before so much as inspecting the cube steak. "I mean —are you happy, Happy?"

"What? Oh, sure," answered Happy absentmindedly. "Miss Catherine, can we practice tonight?"

"Practice what?" said Tucker suspiciously. "Are they training you to roll over and do dopey doggy things like that?"

"Perhaps later we can practice a little," said Miss

Catherine. "When Horatio's gone to bed. But right now, just eat, child. Look"—she tapped a bowl that had HAPPY printed in large red letters on it—"here's that lovely steak bone we've been saving. I decided that today—"

"Practice *what?*" insisted Tucker.

"Just eat, child," said Harry Cat.

They ate.

With much frowning concern—and also a little pleasure—Tucker licked cube-steak juice off his whiskers. "Where have they got you living, Happy? In the storeroom?"

"I'm glad you reminded me, Tucker." With a few expert passes of her tongue, Miss Catherine cleaned her own whiskers. "Is everyone finished? Follow me!" She led them quickly through the hall.

Happy stopped at the door to the music room, then caught up, and whispered excitedly, "Jimmy got through 'The Spinning Wheel,' Miss Catherine!"

"That's nice, dear," the Siamese smiled back.

" 'Dear,' " grumbled Tucker to all and sundry concerned.

"I think my note helped, don't you, Miss Catherine?"

"Oh, I'm sure it did!" The cat winked at Harry. Or perhaps some dust got stuck in her eye.

Happy explained to everyone, almost apologetically, "Jimmy's not one of our very best pupils, you know."

Miss Catherine cleared more dust, or whatever it was, from her throat, and said, as they turned a corner, "Here's our room."

"Our room?" Tucker stopped in his tracks.

"You got quite an echo here!" observed Lulu.

"Shut up, Lulu."

"Of course, at first Horatio wanted him to sleep on *his* bed, but I insisted, and—" With a wave of her paw, Miss Catherine proudly pointed out: "Harry, do you recognize that?"

"I *do* seem to have seen it before."

"My old rug! From the basement. Much too big for a cat, but in a flash it occurred to me it would make a perfect mat for Happy!"

"Mmm!" purred Harry, as pleased as an alley cat can be. "What an excellent idea!"

"Feels pretty hard," said Tucker, jumping up and down on the mat. "I'm surprised you didn't get Horatio down here on the floor while you and Happy—"

"Oh, a hard bed's best—for a growing dog, cat, any-one. The back, you know. My own basket—here it is, by the bye—it may look soft, but just you try jumping in that!"

"Thanks, no, Miss Catherine. In a hope chest I wouldn't jump."

"Well, have a look, anyway," she said gaily. "Go on. I suspect that you'll like what you see. Then I'll tell you another plan that I have."

Tucker reared on his hind legs warily and peered into the basket. The bottom was lined with dark blue velvet and around the edges were necklaces, bracelets, rings glittering. "Very pretty," he had to admit.

"That's *my* collection!" said Miss Catherine. "And what I'd thought was—why don't we exchange? Temporarily, I mean. The way great museums loan out their things."

"I'll think about it," said Tucker Mouse. "Is that ruby real? In that ring there?"

"Indeed it is! It came to Mrs. Smedley from her Great-aunt Agatha, and—"

"I'll think about it."

"If I were you, Kate, I'd get all the stuff insured," said Lulu, "before it goes down to the drainpipe."

"Did Huppy break anything?" asked Harry. "Not your things, Miss Catherine. But Mr. Smedley's heirlooms?"

"A couple of teacups"—she shrugged the damage off. "Just china. We put all the fragile things up on the top shelves of the bookcases."

Happy had been restlessly bouncing around by the door while all this talk of worldly possessions went on. His dance of impatience overcame him at last. He pawed the edge of his mat and pleaded, "Miss Catherine—I think it's time for Barbara Knowles—"

"Not yet," said the Siamese. "She comes at three-thirty and I'll tell you when it's time for Barbara."

163

"But can't I go look? In case she came early? She likes to hear me at the *start* of her lesson! And she always plays better—" His voice trailed off hopefully.

"Then go and look," said Miss Catherine. "But don't interrupt if Jimmy's still there."

"Okay!" Through white fur his blue eyes flashed with importance. "It's just that—well, when I'm on duty I like to be ready for any emergency. And Barbara was making such progress last week!" Drawing himself up to his full woolly two feet, he paraded out the door.

In his absence, Miss Catherine finally allowed herself a good laugh. "As you can see, Happy's proved to be of tremendous assistance. In fact, sometimes he assists so much that Horatio has to shut the door to the music room."

"He's settled in beautifully," said Harry.

"Settled—I'll say!" grumbled Tucker Mouse. "You'd think he never lived anywhere else."

Head hanging, Happy shuffled in and said dejectedly, "Jimmy's still playing 'The Spinning Wheel.'"

"Don't worry, it won't be long," said Miss Catherine. "In the meantime, why don't you show Harry and Tucker your collar?"

"All right. But you have to pull the fur back."

Happy craned his neck up, and Harry Cat, on hind legs, separated the hair with his paws to reveal a silver medal with HAPPY written on one side of it and Mr.

Smedley's name and address on the other. It was hanging from a red leather collar. "It means I'm legal."

"So what are we? Crooks?" said Tucker. "I see it matches Miss Catherine's leash."

"Oh, I have a leash, too!" said the dog. "You want to see my leash?"

"No!"

"We thought of a plaid sweater as well," said Miss Catherine. "But with all that fur it seemed unnecessary."

"I know the feeling," said Tucker.

To make a little quick conversation, Harry asked, "Did the collar itch, Happy? At first?"

"Some. I scratched at it a day. But then I forgot all about it."

"Yeah," sulked Tucker, "you're pretty good at—"

"I think we ought to go," said Harry.

"Oh, must you?" Miss Catherine asked. "You're welcome to stay for supper, too. It's vegetable dinner—we always have vegetable dinner on Tuesdays—but I'm sure there'll be plenty left over."

"No, no," Harry Cat politely declined, as they made their way through the hall to the kitchen.

"You'll stay, though, won't you, Lulu?" said the Siamese. "I know that Horatio's planning to French-fry some potatoes—"

"Groovy!" Lulu Pigeon approved, leading the way, as always, through the air.

At the rear door to the Smedley apartment there was a nervous emptiness: the time when people said good-bye.

Tucker tried one last time. "I suppose you wouldn't want to come down to the drainpipe, Happy, and visit us? For old times' sake?"

Happy shifted from one pair of legs to the other. "Wouldn't you rather come up here? I don't really fit there, you know."

"I guess not," admitted Tucker Mouse.

"Miss Catherine"—Happy peered shyly through his hair—"even if it isn't practice, can I show what I've learned already?"

"All right," she permitted, with frowning reluctance. "But softly now—softly!"

And as softly as a big dog could, Happy howled the opening bars to the sextet from *Lucia di Lammermoor*. Then proudly barked.

"Yup," said Tucker, "it's time to go."

"That was really grand!" said Harry Cat.

The front doorbell to the apartment rang. "There's Barbara!" Happy bounded away.

"Young fellow!" Miss Catherine called. "Aren't you forgetting—"

"What? Oh—" He dashed back and lap-kissed Harry. And lap-kissed Tucker so vigorously the mouse fell on his back. He was gone. From the hall came joyous barking.

Tucker stood up and brushed himself off. "Well, that's something at least, I guess."

"He does so like to be at the door when the pupils arrive," Miss Catherine explained. "A wag of the tail, a lap at the hand, don't you know—it sets the mood for the lesson."

Last goodbyes . . .

But when Harry and Tucker were in the hall, the Siamese stuck her head out the door. "Oh, and, Tucker, remember, Happy can't fit in that drainpipe of yours—but *I* still can!"

"You're welcome any time." The mouse made her a gallant bow.

The two of them were halfway to the street, nine flights—and neither one had said a word—when Harry proposed, "Let's rest a minute." They stopped on a landing. "Okay, Mousiekins—what's wrong?"

"Don't call me Mousiekins."

"You're mad."

"I'm not mad," said Tucker. "I'll tell you why I'm mad! *He doesn't even miss us!*"

"You want him to miss us—?"

"He could miss us a little bit!"

"—and be homesick? And lonely? And miserable?"

"No. I don't want that."

"The whole point was to find him a home. The whole winter long. Wasn't it?"

"Of course."

"And he's found it now. It always feels like a miracle when somebody's found a home in New York. Don't we have ours?"

"Of course we do!"

"Let's go there then. I'm homesick for Times Square. Come on."